Wrangel was on his feet running toward me, shooting wildly. When I caught the vague shadowy bulk of his big body, I fired three times, fast, and threw myself sideways.

In the silence I heard O'Hara's voice,

"What happened?"

"Let's go see," Hardman said. "I think Buel got him."

Wrangel wasn't moving. One of my bullets had caught him in the chest, another had sliced through his belly. The third had missed him completely.

We stood there a moment. Finally I said, "O'Hara, I told you that if he tried again, I'd kill him."

Also by Lee Leighton
Published by Ballantine Books:

CASSIDY

FIGHT FOR THE VALLEY

HANGING AT THE PULPIT ROCK

SUN ON THE WALL

TOMAHAWK

YOU'LL NEVER HANG ME

BEYOND THE PASS

LEE LEIGHTON

BALLANTINE BOOKS • NEW YORK

Library of Congress Catalog Card Number: 56-9443

ISBN 0-345-29219-7

Manufactured in the United States of America

First Ballantine Books Edition:
Second Printing: May 1982

1

IF MY mother had lived, everything might have been different. She was a mild and gentle woman just as my father, Thomas Buel, was a mild and gentle man. Both were unselfish and generous, so generous they never accumulated anything in the way of worldly goods.

Even as a boy I was impatient with my parents. They were never impatient with me because it was not their way, but I knew they were puzzled and often hurt by my attitude and the things I did. I guess I had a talent for trouble, at least by their lights. I left home twice, once when I was fifteen and again when I was seventeen, but I returned both times because my mother was ailing and I didn't have the heart to hurt her any more than I had to.

My father, who was a school teacher, was put upon time after time because he trusted people. My mother was no better. When I protested, she would say, "You've got to trust people, Robert. You can't go through life being cold to everyone you meet."

I wasn't cold, I told myself; just practical. Practical enough to know you couldn't go through life trusting everyone. Only the stupid did that—though my father wasn't stupid. . . . In any case, it was to keep from saying something I would later regret, and to free my father from the burden of feeding me, that I left home.

But I was there the day he received a letter offering him the job of teaching school in Dirken's Hole. He didn't know where the place was. He hadn't even heard of it before. He was offered five dollars a month less than he was getting in this little plains town in eastern Colorado where we had lived for three years, but he took it.

"Don't let him," I told Mother. "He's drifted all his life. There's never been a time I can remember when he's had two silver dollars he could jingle in his pocket."

"Is that important, Robert?" she asked.

"Maybe not, but I know one thing that is. You're not able to make a trip like that. It's a hundred miles on the other side of the front range."

1

She coughed, then wiped the bloody spittle from the corners of her mouth. She leaned against the back of her rocking chair, and smiled at me in her gentle way.

"No, Robert, I'm not able," she said, "but I'm not able to do anything else, either. Thomas knows, and I know, and it's time you were knowing. I won't live through the summer. It doesn't make any difference whether I stay here or travel, and I'd rather travel." She looked out of the window across the prairie to the sand hills that were a lumpy line southward along the horizon. "It's been a long time since I saw the mountains. I'd like to die there."

I said nothing more, realizing she meant what she said. Perhaps it was the reason my father decided to go to Dirken's Hole. We loaded our old, worn furniture into the covered wagon, then waited one more day because the people of the school district had to give my folks a farewell party.

There were speeches and a little gift, a cut-glass sugar bowl and cream pitcher. Handshakes, and some tears that seemed foolish to me, but it had been the same as long as I could remember. People loved my father. Not once had he ever left a school when folks didn't cry because they were losing him.

The next morning we started westward, my mother lying in a bed in the wagon. I rode my buckskin gelding, holding him down to the crawling pace of the wagon. Slowly the mountains grew larger, row upon row of them, the first foothills covered by grass and a few pines, the last row scratching the sky, with Long's Peak rising above the others like a gaunt, snow-capped sentinel.

Then we were in the mountains, climbing slowly, making only a few miles a day, confined by the walls of the canyon through which we labored. My mother by some miracle seemed to be better, perhaps gaining strength from the mountains she had wanted to see again. For an hour or more each night she lay beside the camp fire, listening to the rumble of the creek that poured down the canyon from the snow peaks to the west, and to the whispered message of the aspen leaves.

She would eat a little, then lie back and stare at the sky while the sunlight faded and darkness worked down into the bottom of the canyon and the ridge lines on both sides of us became solid and black against the sky. She would sigh,

2

shivering a little in the piercing chill of the high country, and say, "Put me back. I'm cold."

We topped the divide, crossed a great grass-covered park, and climbed another range, close now to Dirken's Hole. One day we reached the second summit, crossing it by way of Chambers Pass.

At this altitude it was cold, even in August. My mother was chilled, so my father took the wagon on down the western slope, but I remained on top for a time, feeling as if I were God's cousin. This was timber line, with snow packed into the mountain crevices. Just below me a few wind-whipped trees sucked a precarious living from a miserly earth.

On every side of me there was a meadow of tundra grass, the range flattening out. I suppose it was the same tundra that's found in the Arctic, but it was surprising to find it here in the Colorado Rockies. From this high point a man's view was barred only by the great peaks that rose on both sides of the pass. For a moment it seemed to me that time and place were lost in this gray infinity, and suddenly I could not stand it any longer and I hurried after the wagon.

The road leading to Dirken's Hole ran westward, then twisted north, the canyon that held it an apparently bottomless slice in the earth. Far away to the northwest I thought I could see the Hole, probably still two days away.

Actually it was three days. The descent was sharp, the road narrow and crooked and rough, and I wondered if this was the only way into the Hole. If so, it must be snowbound all winter, for Chambers Pass would certainly be closed.

I didn't know how many people lived in the Hole, or what kind they were, but I could imagine what living here would be. No supplies would come in from November until May or June when the hot sun opened the pass; no mail; no news.

Here was a tiny world set aside for those months from the big world that surrounded it. Dirken's Hole might as well be on another planet. Weddings, births, deaths, funerals: all of life would be lived down here in the Hole by a handful of people who knew each other too well, where passions could reach fantastic heights and a man might understandably look with lecherous intent upon his neighbor's wife, driven by the desire to break the monotony of daily life if nothing else. As I thought about it, I wondered not only why my father had

3

come to Dirken's Hole, but why anybody lived here. I was sure of one thing. It wasn't for me.

The third night down from the pass we camped barely inside the Hole, a quiet spot except for the boisterous pounding of the creek. My mother had reached the end of her string. She could not eat at all, and when my father and I had finished, she called us to her. In the twilight she looked gray and thin and old, although she was only thirty-eight.

"My dears." She took one of my hands with her right and one of my father's with her left. "You're nineteen, Robert. You're as big as your father, and strong. You haven't learned to discipline yourself yet, but you will. I don't know what direction you'll take. I do know that whatever it is, you'll go a long way." Then she looked at my father and there was an expression in her eyes that was only for him. "Thomas, I love you. Every day and every hour I've loved you from the moment we were married. I hate to leave you."

Tears poured down my father's face. He could not say anything. Neither could I. I began to shiver, and thought rebelliously how wrong it was for her to die at her age.

"Robert." Her eyes turned to me. "Your father and you have never understood each other very well. You're our son, but different from either of us. Stay with him, Robert. You need each other."

I nodded. I said nothing, for I could not promise, even now. She whispered, "I'm glad I came. It's beautiful."

She died a few minutes later, a smile on her lips.

We buried her the next afternoon above the road where the creek would sing to her each day, and she could listen to the aspen leaves until they turned to fiery orange and fell across her grave. I returned to the wagon, but my father stayed there until dark. When he came back to camp, his face was filled with misery, but he wasn't crying.

"We must not grieve for her," he said. "Whatever is good in the afterlife will be hers, but I can't help feeling sorry for myself and for you. We'll go on to the settlement in the morning." He cleared his throat. "Robert, I'm going to stay here if I can as long as I live."

I looked at him for a moment, a big man with gentle brown eyes, and wondered, Why, of all places where he has lived, does he say that about Dirken's Hole?

4

WE BROKE camp at sunup, leaving the coolness of the high country, and followed the creek out of the aspens into the oppressive heat of the Hole. Here there wasn't even a runty cedar. Just sagebrush, and an occasional patch of grease-wood. On both sides of us I could make out the high rims—impenetrable walls veiled and made hazy by heat waves.

Near the end of the morning we saw the first ranch, a poverty-spread to our right: a log cabin, a slab shed, and a pole corral. A small ditch crossed the road and carried water to a spotty alfalfa field beyond the buildings. Two dirty-faced boys stood in the scant shade of the shed and eyed us as we rode past. They would be in my father's school and he would find a way to help them, even if it meant spending some of his meager salary.

An angular red-faced woman was chopping wood behind the cabin. When she heard us she stopped and, straightening up, leaned on her ax handle and watched us with as much curiosity as her boys showed. She was wearing little, if anything, but a faded calico dress, which clung to her sweaty body.

An hour later we nooned where a stream came in from the west. Later I learned it was Dirken's Creek. The one we had been following from Chambers Pass was July Creek. Here a grove of cottonwoods gave a deep and welcome shade, and for a time after we ate we lay in the grass staring at the sky. I was thinking of my mother, and I'm sure my father was, too. Presently he raised up on one elbow and looked at me.

He said, "Robert, I have a feeling my destiny is here. I can't tell you why, but I do. Regardless of how much I need you, I realize I can't ask you to stay. This is no place for a young man with ambition, so if you want to start back, feel free to go."

He understood me better than I had thought. I was silent for a time. I lay on my side looking at him—the silver fringe along his temples, the network of lines around his eyes, the bold chin that did not indicate anything about his character. A man capable of doing a number of things well, he could have been, if he had chosen, reasonably wealthy by now. But he never would be. He was no more capable of changing, I thought, than the sandstone walls that frowned down upon the valley.

I asked, "Why did you decide to be a school teacher?"

He smiled. "I have expected to hear that question from you for years." He sat up and put his arms around his knees. "I like children. But I'm not sure that's the whole answer. Maybe it's something I know I can do. Or maybe I just don't have the ambition you have."

I knew there was no use pursuing it. Probably he worried about me more than I worried about him. And I couldn't change either. I had to have excitement in my life, action, movement, while my father had chosen a dull career that promised nothing more exciting than wiping a child's dirty nose or wrestling through an algebra lesson with some older pupil who thought he needed a little "higher education."

"Maybe I've got too much ambition," I said. "It's like Ma told me. No telling where it'll take me."

"Don't put it that way," he said sharply. "It shouldn't be a question of where it'll take you, but where you'll take it."

"Sure," I said, irritated, for this was a point he had worn thin long ago. "I'll go on down to the settlement with you. Might as well see what there is to see."

He rose, pleased. I think he would have been happy if I'd said I'd stay here in the Hole with him, but it was something I couldn't do.

"We'd better roll," he said. "May be quite a piece yet."

After we left the cottonwoods, I saw what seemed to be a big and prosperous ranch at the base of the rim to the west, but down here along the creek nothing was either big or prosperous. The places we passed were farms, not ranches—a few cows and pigs and chickens and small grain fields; but obviously the money crop was hay, and I had a hunch that most of it was sold to the ranch next to the rim.

As we rode, I thought about it. No one could afford to haul hay out of the Hole across Chambers Pass, but a herd of cattle could be driven to market every fall. It was my guess that what money came into the country resulted from the sale of cattle.

I wondered if there was only one ranch. I hoped not, for

then the owner would be lord of the valley and he would try to rule my father just like everyone else. My father, for all of his gentleness, was a stubborn man in many ways. He would hold to his principles regardless of the consequences if it came to a test.

The road made a straight line to the north, leaving the creek, which twisted in a great loop to the west. In late afternoon we reached the settlement, which was located in almost the exact center of the valley. The sandstone cliffs to the north were visible now, as were the mountains behind us through which we had come, both farther away than the rims on the east and west. It was a big valley, far bigger but more thinly settled than I had expected.

The settlement was less, too, than I had anticipated, the only pleasant thing about it was the shade from the giant cottonwoods that lined both sides of the road. A rambling log building on our left was the store, probably the only one in the Hole. A bullet-scarred sign across the front read: GENERAL MERCHANDISE AND LIQUORS, PAUL ROME, PROP.

Directly opposite the store was a two-story log house, with a barn and a number of corrals behind it. Beyond was the schoolhouse, which had a shed and two outbuildings in the rear. Still farther down the road I could see another house, a woodshed and barn behind it. That was the settlement in Dirken's Hole, a few weathered buildings made of logs.

My father stopped in front of the store as I reined up and dismounted. He stepped down, tired and dusty. As I tied, he said, "Paul Rome is on the school board. I'll go in and make myself known."

He went inside, and I would have followed if I had not seen the girl leaning against the cottonwood across the road. I had not seen her walk out of the house; I had no idea where she came from, but suddenly she was there, eyeing me with the same frank curiosity the two boys and their mother had shown at the first place we had passed that morning.

I suppose it was natural enough, for strangers would be rare in Dirken's Hole. But this girl was different, a difference I sensed without being able to put my finger on it. She was tall and slender, but not too slender, her pink dress cut to accentuate the curves of breasts and hips. Her black hair hung in a long braid down her back. A red ribbon was tied in a bow at

7

the base of her neck, and it was the ribbon, I think, that gave me the impression she was hardly more than a child.

She said, "Hello."

The word, in the way she said it, was a frank invitation to cross the road and get acquainted, or so I thought. I said, "Hello," and touched the brim of my hat. I walked to her, her dark, bold eyes meeting mine, and I knew I had not mistaken her intent. When I stopped I was within two steps of her, and I saw she was anything but a child. A woman, certainly older than I was, with proud, full breasts pressing against the gingham cloth of her bodice, her skirt short enough to demonstrate that her ankles were trim and exciting.

"Welcome to Dirken's Hole," she said.

I swallowed, sweat breaking out all over me. I wished I had followed my father into the store. Her eyes ran down my lanky body and came back to my face, and she smiled as if she liked what she saw.

Her lips parted, the tip of her tongue slipping out and moistening them. She asked, "Who are you?"

"Bob Buel."

"The school teacher?"

"His son."

"Oh." She looked past me at the wagon and my horse, and nodded. "He's talking to Paul, I suppose. Well, we need a teacher and we never can keep one. I don't blame them. Why anybody lives in this God-forsaken corner of hell is something I don't know."

"Why do you live here?"

"I'm serving my sentence," she said bitterly, motioning toward the house behind her. "That's the hotel. Effie has to have help and I'm it. Effie's the owner. She's an old bat. You'll find out when you live here."

"I'm not going to live here," I said. "I just came with my father to see what it looks like."

"It will be lonesome for your father if you leave," she said. "I can tell you that now. Anybody'd be lonesome here if he ever knew anything else."

"Why do you stay?" I said. "Just because this Effie needs help . . ."

"You don't understand. I'm married to her son. I'm Susan

8

Castle. Effie Castle is my mother-in-law. I call this place Effie's Castle. Funny, isn't it?"

But I didn't laugh. I was sick, way down in my belly. I looked past Susan at the hotel, wondering if her husband would be running out with a gun in his hand. If I had a pretty wife who stood at the edge of the road flirting with every man who came by, I'd lay a hand on her where it would do the most good and I'd gun-whip the man. I didn't propose to stand around and find out whether this Castle fellow had the same idea.

I whirled and started across the road. Susan called, "What's the matter with you?" She ran after me and caught my arm. "I'm not poison."

I jerked free. "Maybe you're not, but your husband might be."

"So that's it. Well, don't worry about him. He's not here. He's a damned horse thief just like his mother and I'm sick and tired of the whole business. All I want is to get out of the Hole." She caught both my arms this time and looked up at me, her face close to mine. She was pretty, terrifyingly pretty, but she was a man trap and I was afraid. She said, "Take me with you when you go. Tonight. In the morning. Any time. I'll steal one of Effie's horses. You'll never regret it."

I jerked free again. "Let me alone," I said, and whirled, and this time I ran.

She didn't follow and I didn't look back. It was the craziest thing that had ever happened to me. You couldn't explain it, a woman throwing herself at a man she had never seen before. Maybe she hated Effie and maybe she hated her husband and I was sure she hated Dirken's Hole, but no sane woman could hate her life enough to throw herself at a man she had never seen before. And to steal a horse to boot . . . !

I was breathing hard when I went into the store. My father was talking to a short bald man who had a white apron tied above the round bulge of his belly. He had a middle-aged look about him, but I didn't think he was over thirty-five.

My father motioned for me to come to him. He said, "Mr. Rome, I want you to meet my son Robert."

"I'm most happy to meet you," Rome said heartily as he shook hands. "If you're looking for a job, I think you can sign on with Skull. It's the only big cow outfit in the valley.

9

You'd have seen it to the west as you came into the Hole."

"Thank you," I said, "but I'll be riding out in the morning. I just came along to help Dad get settled."

"Well, come back whenever you can," Rome said. "We have a fine community and I assure you your father will be well taken care of." He motioned toward the door that led into his saloon. "If you'll step in here, we'll have a drink."

"No, I'll have to turn it down," my father said. "I have no objections to other men drinking, but I have strict ideas about what a teacher should and should not do."

"Very admirable," Rome said. "What about you, Bob?"

I looked at him. His voice had the false ring of a counterfeit dollar. I said, "I guess I'd better not take the time. I've got to help unload the wagon."

"Drop in any time you change your mind," Rome said. "The offer still holds. And don't forget, Mr. Buel. Just give a holler if there is any way we can help."

"I won't forget," my father said, deeply grateful.

That was like him, I thought as we went out. Not once had Paul Rome met my eyes squarely while I was in the store, but it was a thing my father wouldn't have noticed and I saw no reason to call it to his attention.

"The place on the other side of the schoolhouse is the teacherage," my father said as he climbed to the wagon seat. "It's ready to move into, Mr. Rome said."

I mounted, looking at the cottonwoods across the road and then at the hotel, but I saw no sign of Susan Castle. I discovered that I wanted to see her. She had a face and body I would not soon forget.

I pondered that as I rode beside the wagon. I had heard plenty of man-talk in saloons when I was away from home about how you could tell if a woman was any good as soon as you were around her. If she liked it, you knew right away without her saying a word, and if she wasn't worth a damn, you'd know that, too.

I wanted to find out about Susan Castle. . . . I'd better be moving on, I told myself, or I'd wind up swapping smoke with her husband, and for a reason I wouldn't be proud of.

What kind of a damned, poor country was this? I thought of the dirty-faced boys we had seen, of the sweaty, tired woman who was cutting wood, of Susan, of the husband and mother-in-law she had called horse thieves, and of Paul Rome who could not look me in the eyes. My father wouldn't last a year, I thought.

In the morning I shook hands with my father and promised to write to him. I rode away, turning back once to wave, then I was opposite the hotel and I started looking for Susan. I was past it when I saw her come through the door of an outbuilding, her hands smoothing her skirt around her hips. She saw me and waved, calling to me in a friendly tone, but I did not wave or say anything to her. I did not even look back. I was afraid of myself.

I was right about one thing. I did not forget her through the months that followed.

3

DURING THE five years that I was gone from Dirken's Hole, I had all the excitement and action and movement that I wanted, and at times a little more. I drifted south into the San Juan mining country, took a job as night marshal in a gold camp, and after a few months of that, signed on as a deputy sheriff. Later I rode farther south to the border.

I became a bounty chaser simply because it promised more money than I'd ever receive as a lawman unless I made a reputation as a gun fighter, and I had no ambition in that direction. A big man like Wyatt Earp or Bat Masterson could go into a tough community and tame it, naming his salary, but I had seen too many town tamers. They never had a good night's sleep and I liked to sleep.

During the summers I wrote to my father. I never told him much about myself, letting him infer I was punching cows. I received several letters from him each year, anywhere from six weeks to six months old before they caught up with me.

My father stayed in Dirken's Hole just as he said he would. In many ways he was as evasive as I was, but he said he was healthy and happy.

As far as I was concerned, I lived without any real goal except the vague one of some day wanting to own a ranch or a good business in town. Gradually I began to realize how futile my fiddle-footed life was. I kept moving so my enemies would not catch up with me, a safety measure that also prevented me from making any real friends. Although I wasn't aware of it, I was gaining something of a reputation among lawmen, and it was that reputation which eventually sent me back to Dirken's Hole.

When I left the Hole I had no intention of returning, but when I realized my father had meant what he'd said about staying, I made up my mind I would go back. He was all the family I had. Still, I kept putting it off, and I'm not sure I ever would have got around to returning if I hadn't drifted back into Colorado and stopped in Grand Junction, where I ran into Pat Mulvaney. He was the sheriff there and had been the town marshal in Silverton when I had been the night man.

We had a drink, Pat quizzing me about where I had been and what I had done, and all the time I had a notion he was ahead of me with every question and knew the answer before I gave it. Finally I got a little sore. I said, "What the hell, Pat? I'm not wanted by the law, if that's what you're getting at."

He got red in the face and said, "I was just talking. That's all. Just talking." He held his hand out. "I've got to get back to the office. Gonna be around town for a while?"

"Guess so," I said. "I don't have anywhere particular to go."

"Good," he said. "Let's have dinner in the Mesa Hotel. I might have something for you."

"All right," I said.

"Twelve," he said, and I nodded, and he left.

I was in the hotel lobby a few minutes early. At straight-up twelve Mulvaney came in with a little, leathery-faced man who looked as if he had been left out in the desert too long. He was Jason Harwig, Mulvaney said when he introduced us, a name that was vaguely familiar.

The talk was more or less aimless all through the meal, but I saw that Harwig kept sizing me up. I did a little sizing up of my own, too, because I figured he meant to offer me a job. If I was going to work with him, I had to make up my mind about him. I had been a lone wolf too long to jump into a deal without taking a good look first.

Harwig was about fifty, I judged, with big hands for a small man and the pale blue eyes of a killer. He carried a walnut-handled .44 in his holster, and I judged he'd be lightning-fast with it if he had to be, but I didn't think he was

12

merely a paid gun fighter. Mulvaney wouldn't be backing him if he were.

When we finished eating Mulvaney glanced at Harwig, who nodded. Mulvaney said, "Let's go upstairs to Jason's room. He's got a proposition for you."

I didn't quite like the smell of things, but I went with them, mostly because I trusted Mulvaney. The part that bothered me was Jason Harwig's name. I knew I'd heard it and I should be able to place him, but I just couldn't quite put my finger on it.

When we were in Harwig's room, he shut the door, got out a box of cigars and passed them around, then motioned for me to sit down. He said, "Buel, Pat here tells me you're a solid man in a pinch. I've never heard of you, and that's fine because I want a man who isn't known in these parts. Pat says you've been in New Mexico and Arizona lately."

"That's right."

"But you have been in Dirken's Hole?"

The question set me back on my heels. I looked at him, not knowing what he was getting at. I said finally, "I was there five years ago last August."

"Your father's still there?" I nodded and he asked, "Still teaching?"

"Yes, but I——"

"Wait. I've got one more question. Could you go back to see him without anyone wondering why?"

"I guess so," I answered. "I haven't seen him for more than five years and he's been after me to come back."

"Good, good," Harwig said. "I'm done asking questions except for the big one. Would you be interested in spending a winter in Dirken's Hole for two thousand dollars? Or for one thousand?"

I had been holding the cigar in my hand wondering how soon he would get down to brass tacks. Now, when he made the proposition, my memory finally clicked. Jason Harwig was a range detective for the cattlemen's association, a hatchet man, if you want to be honest about it. Harwig came into action when the ordinary ways of handling crime didn't work. I knew nothing about him personally, but I knew his kind and his methods. They weren't mine.

I got up and moved to the window. Mulvaney was standing

13

with his back to the door. Both men were watching me. I lighted my cigar, thinking about two thousand dollars. Even one thousand, with what I had, would be enough to buy a small ranch. I was ready to settle down and I'd like to spend a winter with my father. He wouldn't have changed, but I had, and I wanted to get acquainted with him again. And there was Susan Castle. I hadn't forgotten her, either in my mind or my belly. But she was married. That, as much as anything, decided me.

I said, "No, I guess not."

"Why?" Harwig demanded.

I couldn't tell him about Susan, so I said, "I finally placed you. I'm no Tom Horn."

"Well, by God." Harwig slammed a hand against the bed beside him. "So that's it. You've got a hell of a lot of room to talk, Buel. I've known a few bounty chasers in my life——"

"I'm still no Tom Horn," I said hotly. "It's my guess you are. Besides, my father lives in Dirken's Hole and I'm not going in and raise hell for him."

Harwig was halfway to his feet when Mulvaney stepped to the bed and shoved him back. "Ease up, Jason. Buel's made a good point and you know it or you wouldn't be getting sore. Tell him what the deal is. No reason it would hurt his dad."

Harwig glared at me. Finally he had his temper under control, and he said, "Sure, he made a point, but it gravels the hell out of me to hear a bounty chaser getting high and mighty."

"One thing's sure," I said. "I never brought a man in who wasn't convicted, and I never killed a man while I was bringing him in. Can you say that?"

"No, he can't," Mulvaney said. "That's what put the burr under his tail."

"Aw, go to hell," Harwig said sourly. "I know a few things, too. We ain't gonna have free range much longer. The big outfits are about finished, so they grab at any straw they can. You can't blame 'em for trying to keep what they've got."

"You can blame them for the methods they've used," I shot back. "Tom Horn was the one who got his neck stretched, not the bastards who hired him."

"Give him your proposition," Mulvaney said wearily.

Harwig grunted something and eyed me for a moment. He

14

said, "All right, see how this looks to you. The job's got nothing to do with what you're thinking about. Dirken's Hole is half-outlaw country. It's like a lot of that wilderness up there, off by itself without any law. Folks are honest enough, by their lights anyhow, but they get their hands into outlaw business just the same. They buy stolen stock. They furnish fresh horses to men on the dodge. They'll even buy money that's too hot to spend, maybe for ten cents on the dollar, and save it till they can get rid of it."

He had let his cigar go out. Now he lighted it again, still watching me closely. Then he went on, "This job has two angles. The first one is worth the thousand dollars. A couple of outlaws held up a train out of Rock Springs a piece and stole a pile of dinero, close to fifty thousand. The posse lost 'em just north of the Hole. We figure they're in the Hole now. Your job is to bring 'em out in the spring."

"The other job?"

"It's worth the second thousand. That's to find out who stakes the outlaws to fresh horses and grub. It's all part of the same pattern, but the chances are only two or three are doing it."

"Why don't you go?"

"I've been there," Harwig said. "They know who I am. How about it?"

I still wasn't sure. I had no objections to bringing the outlaws out. The other job was different and I wanted no part of it. I shook my head.

"Not me," I said. "I can't swallow the second deal."

"Take the first one then. It won't be tough. There was only one fellow in the Hole who could be called a bad one, a man named Castle. He was shot and killed a year ago this summer.

"Castle," I said, wondering how many Castles there were in the Hole.

"Link Castle," he said. "Effie Castle was his mother. She runs the hotel."

Then this Link Castle was the one. Susan was a widow! Funny, how all of a sudden this one little fact made a great deal of difference in my thinking. Funny, or crazy. I didn't want to marry her. I wasn't in love with her. You didn't just up and fall in love with a woman by talking to her a minute or so under some cottonwoods on a hot afternoon. Just the same, I had been afraid to go back as long as I'd thought Susan Castle was a married woman.

I didn't want Harwig and Mulvaney to see the pulling and hauling that was going on inside me, so I gave them my back, standing at the window and chewing on my cigar. Presently I asked, "Who are the outlaws I'm after?"

"We don't know," Harwig said. "They were masked."

"Anyone killed in the holdup?"

"No, but one of the trainmen was wounded. He got a pretty good look at them. One was about my size. The other one was tall and slim. The trainman figures the short one was older, but he can't swear to it 'cause he never got a look at the fellow's face."

"Not much to go on," I grumbled. "You can't even be sure they're still in the Hole. They might have ridden out over Chambers Pass by now."

Harwig shook his head. "The posse sent out some wires soon as they got back to Rock Springs. The south end of Chambers Pass has been guarded ever since. Anyhow, these two bastards will stay in the Hole because they know they'll be safe there and can sleep without keeping one eye open."

I took the cigar out of my mouth and turned around to face Harwig. "How do you know Castle was shot and killed?"

He smiled thinly. "I was the one who shot him."

"Are you working for the railroad?"

"Hell no. Railroad and association operatives often work together. Besides, the association is interested in finding out who's helping the outlaws."

Once it found out, I thought, the association would send one of its exterminators into the Hole and there'd be a killing from the brush. I still wanted no part of that, but bringing two train robbers out was another matter.

"All right," I said. "I'll take the job."

I saw no reason to repeat that I'd do one job, but not both, and if Harwig noticed that I had used the singular instead of the plural, he ignored it. "Not much time to spare," he said briskly. "There's some snow on the pass now and there may be more any day. It's up to you to get over it before it's closed. Get your outfit together this afternoon, and I want your picture taken. You'll have to work under cover

16

and get their confidence. Nobody in the Hole will point out your men to you. I'll get some reward dodgers run off for you after we get your picture taken. You'll have to figure out a way to drop one or two where they'll do some good."

I didn't like that and I said so. "There'll be hell to pay if my dad gets his hands on one of them."

"He will," Harwig said. "If somebody finds out something, they all know it. He'll just have to trust you."

I still didn't like it, but I let it go. The trick was an old one, but it had worked with men who should have known better.

When I was ready to go, Harwig handed me several reward dodgers that were frayed around the edges and looked as if they were weather-stained and had been tacked at the corners to a wall or telephone pole. Below my picture were the words: BOB BUEL, ALIAS THE OCHOCO KID, ALIAS BEN BALL. WANTED FOR TRAIN ROBBERY. ONE THOUSAND DOLLARS REWARD.

"You didn't need to make it so good," I grumbled. "Somebody will be taking a shot at me for the reward."

"Nobody in Dirken's Hole," Harwig said.

"Who is this Ochoco Kid?"

"I made the name up," Harwig answered. "Ben Ball was a small-time outlaw in the Northwest who disappeared about a year ago. Actually he was killed, but that ain't generally known."

"Suppose these men knew Ben Ball? Or heard of me?"

"Those are risks you've got to take," Harwig admitted, "but it ain't likely either one will trip you up. You can claim you've been on the Pacific Coast and this Bob Buel who's been chasing wanted men along the border is a different man. The majority of these bastards who operate north of here are Montana and Wyoming men who don't get down to the border. Or out to the Northwest, either."

I shook hands with him, and rode out of town, leading my bed horse. I still didn't like it, but I didn't have to use the reward dodgers if I didn't want to, so I put them out of my mind.

My thoughts turned to my father. Somehow I couldn't imagine him staying this long in what Jason Harwig called

17

"half-outlaw country." He simply wouldn't fit unless he had changed.

I knew this "half-outlaw" society and its code: if the bandits didn't bother you, you didn't bother them. They were Robin Hoods of a sort, stealing from the rich. In the minds of many small settlers it was always open season on cattle syndicates, railroads, and banks. But for my father to adopt such an attitude was inconceivable. He would keep my secret if I had to tell him why I was there. I was sure of it.

Snow was early, the big snow which would ordinarily not have fallen until well into November. This time I did not tarry on Chambers Pass. For miles on both sides I rode through the worst storm I had ever seen. For a time I wasn't sure I'd make it. After I had, I was sure I would be the last man over the pass this year.

I stopped at my mother's grave, finding a fence around it and a marker bearing her name and the dates of her birth and her death. I stood there for a long time, the naked aspen limbs above me, a few withered leaves on her grave under the thin covering of snow, and it shocked me that there was no sign my father had been here for months.

There was little change in the valley. The farms I passed were as poverty-stricken as I had remembered them; the big spread on my left that Paul Rome had called Skull looked as prosperous as ever; and when I reached the settlement, I found no change there.

As I passed the hotel, I studied it, wondering if Susan Castle was still there. Probably not, feeling as she had toward her mother-in-law. She was living alone, probably. Or she had left the valley. I could not forget how violently she hated it and how she had begged me to take her with me.

In a way the thought that she had left the Hole comforted me. I didn't understand my feelings. I wanted to see her and yet I didn't want to.

I reined up in front of the teacherage, seeing nothing of my father. It was late afternoon, the light beginning to fade. He was in the house, probably reading, I thought. I opened the door, thinking I would surprise him. But he wasn't in the front room.

I went on into the kitchen and stood there, frozen. My father wasn't here, either, but a woman was, a tall, slender

18

woman who was bending over the stove looking at something in the oven. She shut the oven door and looked around; I recognized her before she turned. Susan Castle!

"Why, Robert," she said as if pleased and not nearly as shocked as I was. "Your father said all the time you would come like this, surprising us." She crossed the kitchen to me and kissed me. "Welcome home."

"What are you doing here?"

She smiled. "I thought you knew. Your father and me were married last June."

4

I DON'T know how long I stood there staring at her. I simply could not believe it. In the first place I was unable to accept the fact that my father had married again. But to have married Susan Castle, young enough to be his daughter, the kind of woman I was sure she was . . . ! I couldn't believe it—yet here she was.

Finally I was able to ask, "Why did you marry him?"

I'm certain she caught the hostility that I could not keep out of my voice. Her smile faded. Still, she stood there, her eyes searching mine. She looked older than she should have. Pretty enough yet, but a little faded compared to the picture that had been in my mind for five years. Now, as she stared at me, her face very grave, I saw the lines of discontent that marked her forehead.

"I could tell you I love him," she said after a long silence.

"But you don't," I shot at her.

She turned and walked to the bracket lamp on the wall above the stove, touched a match to the wick, tipped the reflector so it threw the light where she wanted it, and opened the oven door again. She looked inside, closed it, then filled the fire box with wood. Suddenly she whirled, the fury that had been mounting in her pouring out in words that sounded as if she had dipped each one in venom before speaking it.

"I'd give anything I've got or ever will get to ride out of this hell hole. But I'm a prisoner like everybody else. I was sixteen when Link Castle found me in Rock Springs and married me. I've been here ever since. If I'd known what it was like, I'd never have married him, but after he brought

19

me here, I was here to stay. When he got plugged, he didn't leave me a penny. That old bitch of an Effie got it all. I kept on working in the hotel. Had to. No one else in the Hole would give me a job."

She stopped, out of breath, or maybe she was so wound up in her feelings she couldn't say any more. She turned her back to me and stood there at the stove. Outside the twilight had become darkness, and a wind had come up, making a thin cry around the eaves.

Whatever strange hold this woman had had upon me for so long was broken. I hated her, hated her because she was here in my mother's place, sharing my father's bed.

Finally she turned and walked across the kitchen to me. She said, "All right, I'll tell you why I married him. I wanted to get out of the hotel. I wanted my own home. I wanted the respectability he could give me." She stopped, her hands tight fists at her sides, then she went on, "And maybe you'd like to know why he married me. I can tell you that, too. He wanted a housekeeper. And . . . and I guess he felt sorry for me."

She stood close to me, her head tipped back, and now she put her hands on my shoulders, saying softly, "Don't hate me, Bob. Please. I can't stand it if you do. I've never forgotten you. Not once from that one little time I saw you. Your father always said you would come back and I knew you would. I guess that was another reason I married him. I wanted to be here when you came."

I backed away, pushing her arms from me. "Where's Dad?"

If she resented my action, she didn't show it. She said, "He rode over to Oren's place after school to get a milk cow." She whirled and walked to the stove, her heels clicking sharply on the floor, the only release she allowed her temper.

"Is there a lantern in the shed?"

"Yes."

I left the house and led my horses to the shed, found the lantern and lighted it. I watered the horses, tied them in two vacant stalls, and fed them; then I waited, smoking one cigarette after another. I couldn't understand it. There was no use even to try, for I could not tell what was in my father's heart.

But what about Susan? She must know he had no money

20

and never would have. He was a middle-aged man who would not be likely ever to take her out of Dirken's Hole. Then I wondered if she actually wanted to leave as much as she pretended? Surely she could have found some way to get out when Link Castle was killed if it was so important to her.

Then I got to thinking about myself. I had looked forward to living with my father, confident he had not changed and equally confident that I had matured enough to find some common ground with him. If I stayed I would be free to ride anywhere in the Hole without arousing suspicion. Sooner or later I would find my men, and I wouldn't have to worry about them getting away from me until the snow melted in the spring.

Now I'd have to figure something else out. I simply couldn't stay in the same house with my father's wife.

I heard him coming. I waited in the doorway, the lantern hanging from a nail behind and above me so he was unable to see my face. As he dismounted, I said, "How are you, Dad?"

For a moment he stood in silence beside his horse, holding the rope with which he was leading the milk cow, then he let out a whoop. "Robert," he shouted, and came to me, his hand extended. I backed up so the lantern light fell directly across his face. I shook hands with him, so shocked by his appearance that I couldn't say anything for a minute. His hair had turned white, his face was thin and was so deeply lined that he looked sixty instead of forty-five.

"Robert, I've prayed for you to come back," he said. "I knew you would some day, but I didn't think it would be this year, the way it's been snowing up there on the pass."

"I didn't any more than make it," I said, and put my hand on his shoulder. "How have you been?"

"Fine, fine," he said with exaggerated heartiness. "I guess you've met my wife if you've been in the house. She's a fine woman, Robert."

I looked at him closely, wondering if he really thought she was a fine woman. It wouldn't be hard to fool him, trusting as he was.

He led the cow into the shed and tied her in a stall, then put his horse away. "I've got to go into the house to get a bucket," he said. "Want to come with me?"

21

"No, I'll wait here," I said.

I stood in the doorway of the barn while he plodded across the yard to the house; I saw the flare of light on the back porch as he opened the door, then it was gone and I heard the door slam. What had happened to him? Teaching had never been a strain on him. Five years of ordinary living could not have lined his face that way or turned his hair white.

When he returned, he said, "I hope you intended to stay here all winter. Not much chance of you getting out until summer."

"Intended to stay," I said carefully. "Suppose I can find any work hereabouts?"

"It's doubtful," he said. "We have one big cattle ranch in the Hole and a sheep ranch at the other end on the east side. Belongs to a man named O'Hara. He's about the most Irish Irishman you ever saw. But they don't hire anybody in the winter. Next summer it will be different."

"I don't figure to be here next summer."

"Stay here and help me with the chores," he said. "I've been farming a little the last year or two. I own a few head of cattle and some horses. I've got a sow and a litter of pigs. About seventy hens and eight geese." He looked at me and laughed, and for the first time I had a glimpse of the man I remembered. "Surprised, aren't you? Well, I thought as long as I intended to stay here I might as well add a little to my salary."

He picked up a one-legged stool and began to milk. I squatted behind the cow, my back to the wall, and I thought how wrong I had been. Dad had never had two silver dollars he could jingle in his pocket. And I had thought that was important. Only one thing was important and I had lacked the sense to see it. He had been happy.

Presently he finished, the foam standing a full two inches above the rim of the bucket. I asked as casually as I could, "Is there any way out of the valley except over Chambers Pass?"

He started to reach for the lantern, and stopped, his hand in mid-air. "Why?"

"Just curious."

He took the lantern down from the nail. "Yes. Or I should say there is a way in. They call it the bandit trail. Those

22

who know it follow a series of ledges into the Hole from the north. I never heard of anyone going out that way. Pretty tricky even coming in. If a man has a horse trained to do it, he can jump him from one ledge to another, but teaching him to jump up a six-foot precipice is a different proposition."

"It's easier to teach a horse to be a cat than a bird," I said. "That it?"

"That's it exactly. You weren't figuring on trying to get out that way?"

"No. My horse doesn't have wings, either." I followed him outside and he shut the barn door. "Will we get snow down here in the Hole?"

"Not this early," he answered. "Along in December, maybe. A lot of difference in altitude between here and Chambers Pass, you know."

As we started toward the house, I asked, "What happens to the creek that goes through the valley? It must get out somewhere."

"No, it doesn't," he said. "Funny thing. North of here the creek begins to peter out. Then it just disappears. Some folks think it comes out as a spring in the desert west of the Hole."

We were almost to the back door when I asked, "Are there any strangers in the valley?"

He stopped and raised the lantern to look at me. "Why, Robert?"

I knew at once I had made a mistake. I could have saved the question until later, but it was what had brought me here and I wanted the answer. I had not even considered the possibility that I should be careful in what I said to my father. I was that sure he had not changed. Even the white hair and the lines in his face had not warned me.

Now, standing there with the bucket of milk in one hand and the half-raised lantern in the other, he kept his eyes on me while he waited for an answer to his question.

"No reason; just occurred to me that in an isolated place like this a stranger would stand out like a boil on your nose."

"That's right," he said heavily. "Well, there are a couple of strangers in the Hole. They showed up about ten days ago —Sam Logan and Eli Hardman."

He went on into the house. I followed, hoping the satisfaction I felt did not show in my face. Logan and Hardman would be my men, and if the trail to the north was as tough as my father said, I could safely wait until spring to take them, just as I had planned.

Supper was ready and we sat down as soon as we washed. I discovered to my surprise that Susan was a good cook. I stuffed myself, for I had not eaten since morning. Susan watched me covertly, smiling slightly. She was wearing a frilly pink apron, tied in a double bow behind her waist, and I could not keep from admitting to myself, grudgingly though it was, that she was one of the most attractive women I had ever seen. When she rose to fill our coffee cups from the pot on the stove, she walked with quick, fluid grace, glancing at me to see if I was watching. I pretended not to be, but I knew she wasn't fooled for a minute.

When we finished, I leaned back in my chair to smoke a cigarette. Susan said, "Tom, this is Friday. You haven't forgotten that the dance is tomorrow night?"

He looked up from his coffee cup, his face clearly showing his misery. "Susan, you know I can't dance. After I hurt my knee haying last summer, I can't even go through the motions."

She knew, all right, and she hadn't forgotten. She was still smiling, her dark eyes locked with mine for just a moment, then they swung back to my father's face. She wants to hurt him, I thought. But why?

"I'm sorry," she said. "I forgot all about your knee. But Robert could take me, couldn't he?"

"Of course." My father's face brightened. "You'll have a good time, Robert, and it will give you a chance to get acquainted with the neighbors. Good people, most of them, aren't they, dear?"

Susan nodded. "All but Billy Wrangel. Why somebody doesn't shoot him is more than I can understand."

"He's a bad one," my father conceded. "He's Mike O'Hara's sheepherder. He fights just for the love of fighting, I guess."

Susan was leaning forward, paying no attention to what my father had been saying. She gripped the edge of the table, her eager brown eyes meeting mine. "You will take me, won't you, Bob?"

I had every intention of saying no because I knew it would

24

be a mistake. If I took her to a dance, I'd set every tongue wagging in the Hole. No, it wouldn't do. In the long run I could see nothing but disaster.

Still, I had no excuse for turning her down. Besides, I would have a chance to look Hardman and Logan over. "All right," I said, "I'll take you."

She laughed lightly, mocking me as if she had known all the time she had my tail in a crack.

5

So, on Saturday night, I took my stepmother to the dance. Susan Castle Buel, twenty-six years old, wearing a white frilly dress that was far too revealing at the neck, walking very close to me, her arm slipped through mine as if to show everyone in the Hole that I belonged to her. Before we reached the store, I was convinced this was the most completely wrong thing I had ever done.

When we reached the store, I found that almost everyone in the Hole was there. Jesse Carter, who owned Skull, drove up with his wife just as we arrived; Skull's crew, riding two abreast at a respectful distance behind their boss, were like the entourage of a feudal lord.

Carter was big in more ways than one. He must have weighed better than three hundred pounds, and his wife, oddly enough, was an attractive, hummingbird kind of woman who probably didn't weigh one-third as much. They came in the strangest-looking rig I had ever seen, a buckboard without a bed, just a wide spring seat placed in the exact center and an iron rail.

Susan stopped at the base of the outside stairway until Carter and his wife stepped down. When she introduced us, Carter's huge hand engulfed mine as he said in a booming voice, "Tom Buel's boy? Well now, son, you favor him, you favor him a lot."

And Mrs. Carter, a little spitefully, I thought, "It was so nice you could bring Susan. Your father forgets she's a young woman."

We climbed the stairs to the big room over Paul Rome's store. Within a few minutes Susan had introduced me to practically everyone, so many names and faces that I was completely confused, but I was sure of one thing. Sam Logan and Eli Hardman were not among the men I met.

Paul Rome, who claimed that he remembered me; Dale Oren, a ruddy-faced farmer who had sold my father the milk cow; Russ Musil, Dick Smith and the rest of the farmers; Bud Stivers, Carter's foreman, and the cowboys who made up the Skull crew.

But the one who stood out to me was Mike O'Hara, the sheepman. His hair was brown, but his thick short beard and pointed mustache were fiery red. He looked like a cutlass-swinging pirate who might order all of us to walk the plank.

O'Hara was no taller than Susan, but he was stocky, with big arms and a thick neck. He slammed me on the back with a heavy hand. "Welcome to Dirken's Hole, Buel. If you're anything like Tom, you're all wool and a yard wide. All wool! You hear? All wool!" A great laugh shook him clear down to his belly. "Say, I want you to meet my girl." He wheeled and motioned with his hand. "Judy. Come here, Judy."

"We haven't got time, Mike," Susan said. "I think we're ready to start."

"I'll dance with you, Susie." He looked at her the way a man looks at only one kind of woman, then he said. "Hell, girl, there's two men here for every woman. You won't miss a dance."

For a moment Susan's face was contorted by a flash of fury, but she controlled her temper. Before she could think of a cutting retort, Judy O'Hara was standing in front of me, a small girl, nineteen or twenty, with hair as red as her father's beard.

"Here's a man for you, Judy," O'Hara said, grinning. "Tom Buel's son just got over the pass ahead of the storm. Now he's trapped for the winter." He winked ponderously at me. "And before spring gets here, she'll have you trapped."

Judy held her hand out to me, blue eyes twin wells of good humor. "Mike doesn't mean a word of it, Mr. Buel. He talks that way, but he's really scared I will get a man and he'll lose a housekeeper."

"No such thing," O'Hara said. "Time I had some grand-sons."

An old man who sat in the corner next to the long table

26

that was loaded with cakes and sandwiches began to tune up his fiddle, and Jesse Carter called, "Get your partners, gents. We're a-wasting time."

O'Hara grabbed Susan's arm. "Let's give it a whirl, Susie. That fiddle is starting my feet to stompin'."

Susan was as helpless as a calf being dragged to a branding fire. She looked back at me, but I pretended I didn't see her. A big man was crossing the floor toward Judy. When she saw him, she said hurriedly, "That's our herder, Billy Wrangel. I don't want to dance with him."

"You don't have to," I said. "I'm here."

I didn't miss a dance with Judy until midnight, when we stopped to eat. During that time the children had gone to sleep, most of them laid out on benches that surrounded the room, or if they were small, bedded down in clothes baskets on the floor. One, the Oren baby Judy said, awoke, and his mother lifted him from the basket and began to nurse him, all the time carrying on a gossipy conversation with Mrs. Carter. Occasionally Mrs. Oren stopped and glanced at Susan, then she'd get her hand back up to her mouth and go right on. For the first time I felt some sympathy for Susan. I noticed that she never visited with any of the other women. I doubted that marrying my father had given her the respectability she had frankly said she sought.

Once, between sets while Judy was wiping her face with her handkerchief, she said, "Your father is a wonderful teacher. I finished the eighth grade the first year he was here." She laughed. "Everybody loves him but I love him the most. He said I was the smartest student he ever had. I suppose he says that to every child who graduates from the eighth grade."

"No, he's too truthful to do that." I glanced at Susan, who was talking animatedly to Paul Rome, and wondered if I was lying. "Has he been happy since he married her?"

The question was a stupid one. It just popped out because it had been in my mind from the moment I had found Susan in my father's house.

Judy gave me a sharp look, and there was a moment of embarrassed silence before she said, "Ask him." I was relieved to hear Uncle Sim's fiddle start up and Jesse Carter call, "All right, ladies and gents, here we go."

Billy Wrangel stood with his back to the wall, a heavy-featured man who looked like a cross between a gorilla and a bull. I don't believe he took his eyes off Judy once from the time the dance started until we stopped to eat. I had a hunch I was in for it, partly because my father had said Wrangel liked to fight, and partly because of the thunderhead look on his face. I sensed, too, that Judy was afraid of him. I wondered if her father knew it, and why he kept Wrangel on his payroll if he did.

Wrangel made no move to interfere or claim Judy for a dance. He just stood there watching, and presently I was able to forget him. I don't believe I ever worked harder in my life than I did that night, or had a better time. Everyone danced with the exaggerated exuberance of people who have few good times. It would go on until sunup, I knew, and I was more than ready to stop at midnight and eat.

Judy showed no inclination to look elsewhere. When Carter's foreman, young Bud Stivers, came to ask her to eat with him, she put her hand on my arm, and said as if she regretted it keenly, "I'm sorry, Bud, but I'm eating with Mr. Buel."

As Stivers turned away, I heard Paul Rome say, "This storm sure caught me with my pants unbuttoned. Three freight wagons on the other side of the pass mired down in this damned snow."

Judy smiled at me wryly. "He's getting ready," she whispered. "About March he'll raise every price in the store."

After I had eaten more sandwiches than I was willing to count, and three pieces of cake and two cups of coffee, Judy said, "I'd like some fresh air. Wait till I get my coat."

She was gone less than a minute, but it was long enough for Susan to cross the room to me. "You fool," she said in a low tone. "I told you last night what Billy Wrangel is." She was thoroughly angry. "Wrangel will half-kill you," she said.

"I'll take care of myself."

"Well, you aren't taking care of me. You haven't danced with me once!"

Judy was there then, buttoning her coat and smiling at Susan. We forced our way through the crowd of wallflowers that formed a solid mass in front of the door. I looked over my shoulder and saw that Wrangel was following. At the foot of the stairs I glanced back. He was standing on the landing staring down at us.

I suppose we walked fifty yards before Judy said, "I wanted to talk to you and I couldn't do it back there. It's been more than five years since you saw your father, hasn't it?"

"Yes."

"Has he changed?"

"More than I could have believed possible. He's aged fifteen years in five."

"In six months," she said with sudden bitterness. "Why did you come, Mr. Buel?"

"To see Dad."

"But why at this time of year? You must have known you'd be snowed in."

I was a little irritated, not quite knowing what she was driving at and afraid she had guessed the truth. I said, "This is a good place to winter. I was out of a job. It isn't easy to find one this time of year."

"You didn't know he was married?"

"No."

She was silent again for a dozen steps or more, then she said, "Let's go back."

We swung around. Irritated, I said, "You didn't get me out here just for some air. What did you aim to tell me?"

"I can't say it," she said miserably. "I thought I could, but I can't. It's something you've got to find out for yourself. And you will, living there in the same house with her." She reached out and touched my arm. "I'm glad you're here. He needs you."

I should have respected her for her reluctance to gossip. Still, she had started something she hadn't finished, and now all my worries about my father swept through me again. I said roughly, "You'd better say what you started to. If there's something about Susan or Dad I should know that I don't, you ought to tell me." But she said nothing.

I liked her, and I didn't want it to be this way between us. Finding a girl like Judy O'Hara in Dirken's Hole was more good luck than I had any right to expect. If I was to be stuck here this winter, I wanted to see her. I had even thought of asking her if I could ride home with her. But here we were, walking side by side as stiff and cold as two icicles.

We had almost reached the store, the lighted lantern hang-

29

ing at the foot of the stairs directly ahead of us, when she said, "Mr. Buel . . ."

"Bob."

"All right, Bob. What I wanted to say was that we're a strange community. The rules people live by outside don't apply here. There aren't many of us and we know each other too well. By spring we're all kind of sick. With cabin fever, I guess. We've got to get along or somebody will get killed, so we swallow our pride and do what we can to prevent trouble, but Susan doesn't pay any attention to our rules. Trouble is meat and drink to her."

I didn't know what to say, and before I thought of anything, she went on, "Take Mike and Jesse Carter. Anywhere else a cowman and sheepman would be shooting at each other, but they've lived here for years and never had any trouble. We don't have a lawman or a jail or a judge. We don't have any crime. By our poeple, I mean. We have some outlaws now and then, and we put up with them, but we don't like them."

When she paused, I asked, "What's this got to do with Susan and my father?"

"Everything. Here in the Hole we get along by keeping out of each other's business. We talk about it. I guess it's the only recreation some women like Mrs. Oren have, but we don't interfere. We knew your father was making a mistake when he married Susan, but we didn't try to stop him. I don't suppose you can help him, but at least you can be careful not to make it worse."

I didn't know what she meant. At least I didn't want to believe what I thought she meant. I said, "You're trying to tell me not to live there with them. That it?"

"That's it," she said.

We were in front of the store. No one was in sight until Billy Wrangel stepped out of the shadows. I had forgotten all about him. Judy had, too, I think. She cried, "Billy, I told you to quit spying on me."

"And I told you to quit walking out of the dances with men," he said. "Now I'm gonna bust him. I'm gonna bust him good."

"Billy, stop it."

He shuffled toward me, acting as if he hadn't heard, his big head tipped forward. Judy ran to him, saying something

I didn't catch, but he shoved her out of his way, sending her sprawling, and charged me like a berserk bull. He was almost on me before I saw the singletree in his hand.

He raised it like a club, aiming to kill me with it. I heard Judy scream, "I'm going after Dad, Billy." She ran up the stairs. After that I saw nothing but Billy Wrangel, for I was fighting for my life.

6

THE NIGHT was a dark one, the only light coming from the lantern that hung at the base of the stairs. Sheer instinct made me duck as Wrangel swung the singletree at my head. The club would have cracked my skull if it had landed, and that was exactly what he intended to do. He was a madman, an animal, and I fought him for what he was.

That wild swinging blow carried him half-around and took him off balance. I rushed him, getting him in the belly with a right, then in the face with a looping left that knocked him down. I jumped on him, my boots grinding into his chest and smashing a grunt out of him. He grabbed me by an ankle and I fell headlong on past him, landing flat on my face.

He could not keep his grip on my ankle. I yanked free and scrambled ahead, crablike; if he got his hands on that single-tree again, the chances were he wouldn't miss a second time. But when I regained my feet and turned to face him I saw that he was getting up slowly as if he was dazed.

I drove at him again, hitting him with rights and lefts, vaguely aware that men were streaming down the stairs. A jumbled chorus of yells reached my ears, calling for Wrangel to finish me. Natural enough, for Wrangel belonged in the Hole and I was the outsider, but it added to my fury. They were a pack of wolves hungering for blood, and if there was a single friendly voice among them, it did not reach my ears.

I don't know how long we stood there face to face, stirring the dust as we slowly turned clockwise, each intent on hammering the other into the dust. At first Wrangel had cursed me, but not now. He was sobbing for breath. I had pounded him in the belly and chest until it must have been torture every time he sucked air into his lungs.

I was taking punishment, too. He concentrated on my head, lashing out with clublike blows, but much of the steam was gone. I had taken it out of him that first minute when I gave him my boots. As it was, he worked my face over until it felt like raw meat. One eye was closed. My nose was dripping blood. The right side of my mouth was bruised and swollen.

He backed up, fighting by instinct. I kept on him, but my own strength was going fast. I had been in more fights than I could remember since I was a kid, but I had never been hurt so much in so short a time.

Suddenly he dropped forward, his great arms circling my waist. I couldn't backtrack fast enough. He brought me down and we rolled over and over in the dirt, both of us using our knees and elbows. Now his greater strength was an advantage. He tried for my left eye, a thumb driving down like a hammer and missing by an inch, striking me on the cheekbone. I slammed my knee into his crotch, and he cried out in agony. His grip suddenly relaxed, and I fell away and scrambled to my feet. He got to his hands and knees and looked up at me as if he had to wait for strength to flow into his legs. I should have kicked him in the face: I wanted to but I couldn't move.

My heart was hammering, my blood pounding against my temples; blood and sweat ran down my face and into my mouth. For that one frantic moment I stood there, panting, staring down at his unprotected face, the most inviting target I had ever seen. Then he labored to his feet and once more drove at me, slowly and ponderously, a wounded bear not quite finished. Again he fell forward, holding to me and trying to pull me down again, but this time I held him up.

He battered me in the ribs with his left fist, his right arm around me, his face pressed against my chest. I grabbed a handful of hair, yanked his head back and hit him on the chin, once and then again, short punches that had all my strength in them. I felt the shock of the blows travel up my arm, and I knew I had finished it. His right arm slid away from me, and when I stepped back, taking my support away from him, he fell on his face and did not move.

I had sense enough to get my back against the front of the store and brace my feet in front of me. I leaned there, fighting for breath, my head tipped forward. The crowd seemed stunned, then someone, O'Hara I think, said, "Well, by God,

I wouldn't have believed it." And someone else, "Say, look at that singletree. Buel must have clubbed him with it."

"Sure he did," another man shouted. "Nobody can lick Billy Wrangel with his fists. Let's teach this dirty bastard to fight fair."

I heard the growl come out of them, a sullen, animal-like sound, and Judy, pressed against the foot of the stairs, cried, "Stop it. Billy used the singletree, not Buel. Mike, have you lost all your sense?"

They didn't hear. I was a rabbit, cornered, the fight gone out of me, able to hold myself upright and that was all, but my brain was clear enough, clear enough to know that the crowd was just as dangerous as Billy Wrangel had been a few minutes before.

They moved toward me, O'Hara in front, menacing and silent, and again Judy screamed. I wiped blood from my mouth with my sleeve. I forced my battered lips to say, "He tried to kill me with the singletree. I didn't touch it."

They heard me, but they didn't believe. They were insane, gripped by mob madness. I don't know what would have happened if Judy hadn't broken through the crowd and ran to me.

She put her back against me, throwing out an arm in a repelling motion to the crowd. "You know what Billy is. He fights because he likes to fight. He had no excuse for this. I asked Buel to take me outside for some fresh air. That's all. Billy had the singletree. Can't you get that through your heads?"

They stopped, O'Hara scratching his nose, then pulling at his beard. A man laughed from outside the circle, somewhere on the other side of the road toward the hotel, then I heard a gun being cocked. He said, "If you ain't a bunch of yellow dogs. You don't love Wrangel. Not none of you. If you wasn't scared of him, O'Hara, you'd fire him."

O'Hara bristled. "That's a lie, Hardman. It's just that we like our fights fair, and clubbing a man with a singletree ain't fair."

"But it's fair if Wrangel uses it, I suppose," the man said contemptuously.

"We don't know——" Bud Stivers began.

"You heard what Judy said," the man interrupted. "You calling her a liar?"

"No, but——"

"All right. Wrangel had the singletree. I seen it. So did Sam here. We watched the start of it. A good fight, too. How about it, Sam?"

"That's right," another man said. "Wrangel tried to knock his head off with that singletree."

"Trouble with you boys is that your pride's hurt," Hardman went on. "None of you can lick Wrangel, so you're sore because a stranger came in and done the job."

"That ain't so," O'Hara said hotly. "Wrangel always fought fair. I don't believe——"

"Now you're calling me and Sam liars along with your own girl," the man said. "I don't favor that, so just to be real sure I heard right, say it over."

From the landing at the head of the stairs Jesse Carter called, "This here a dance, or ain't it?"

"Come on," Bud Stivers said. "Wrangel's coming out of it, Mike. No harm done."

They started up the stairs, laughing and pushing, the tension gone. I said, "O'Hara."

He turned toward me uncertainly. "Well?"

He stood with the lantern light on his face, still only half-convinced, I think, that I hadn't used the club on Wrangel. I said, "You're a fool or you're blind, or both, or you wouldn't keep a man on your payroll that your own girl is afraid of."

Startled, O'Hara looked at Judy. "That true?"

"It's true," she said. "I didn't want to dance with him to-night. It made him mad."

"That's nothing to get your hair curly over," he muttered. "Let's go home. The fun's gone."

O'Hara turned to Wrangel and helped him to his feet. Judy said, "I've got to go. I'm sorry this happened."

Still I stayed there, my back against the front wall of the store, sick with a dull, steady ache that seemed to come from every part of my body. I watched O'Hara help Wrangel into the saddle, then he and Judy mounted and the three of them rode away.

The men across the road disappeared. Hardman and Logan, of course, and I wondered why they hadn't come to the dance,

34

and why they had taken my side against the crowd. A hell of a note, I thought, remembering why they were here and why I had come to the Hole.

Maybe Hardman and Logan had saved my life. I couldn't be sure, for there was no way of knowing what the crowd would have done, or whether Judy could have held them off. I'd take both men in, I told myself, regardless of the personal debt I owed them. And I had learned something about the Hole people I had better remember. They held together against an outsider regardless of their own differences.

I don't know how long I stayed there, wondering if I had enough starch in my legs to walk to my father's house. No one had been concerned about me. If Wrangel had clubbed me to death, nothing would have happened to him. A hell of a place to winter, I thought.

They were dancing again upstairs. I heard the thump of feet, the fiddle music, and Jesse Carter's great voice doing the calling. Suddenly Susan appeared out of the darkness. I don't know how long she had been there, or where she had come from. I had supposed she was upstairs with the rest of the women.

"Let's go home," Susan said. "You've had your fun. Now they'll hate you just like they do Hardman and Logan."

She wasn't worried about me. She was sore because I'd danced with Judy, just as sore as Wrangel was. For a moment the thought was in my mind that she might in some way have been back of the fight. She might have needled Wrangel into tackling me, but Wrangel probably hadn't required any needling.

I stepped away from the wall of the store and the ground began to tilt and whirl. She put an arm around me, asking, "You think I'd better get the wagon? Tom will still be up."

I said, "No."

But I was thankful for her support and I leaned on her more than I should have, though once I got started the dizziness left me.

When we went into the house, my father was sitting by the stove reading. He looked at me, shocked by my appearance, and got up. "What happened?" he asked.

"He had a fight with Billy Wrangel," Susan said. "Take the lamp into the bedroom."

35

I followed him, Susan drawing her arm away from me. When I reached the bed I fell across it. I don't believe I could have gone another step. My father pulled off my boots, then he said, "I should have warned you more strongly than I did. Wrangel's a bad one."

I didn't say anything. He was thinking, I suppose, that I had a talent for trouble just as I'd always had, but I didn't intend for it to be that way. Not ever again. Susan came in with a pan of hot water and some clean cloths. She washed my face, being very gentle while my father watched, standing helplessly beside the bed.

"He'll be all right," Susan said, standing up.

I said, "Thank you," and looked at her.

Her face did not soften. "If you want me during the night," she said, "you can call," and left the room.

My father remained there. I said, "I hope this won't hurt your standing in the valley."

"Hurt me?" He rubbed a hand across his face as though he was very tired. "No, nothing you could do can hurt me, Robert. I don't know exactly how it happened, but I have hurt myself."

He blew out the lamp and left the room. I lay on my back, my one good eye open, and I thought about what Judy had told me. Susan was a stray, and maybe my father had taken himself outside the circle when he had married her. The Hole people lived by their own rules, Judy had said. Well, I had mine, too, and my father had his, and maybe I could help him just by being here with him.

But in the spring when I took Eli Hardman and Sam Logan out of the Hole to stand trial, I would kick the roof in on both of us. I would break a rule, probably the number one rule. *They never bothered the outlaws who wintered here if the outlaws didn't bother them.*

The sun was up before I went to sleep. I hurt all over, but it wasn't the pain that kept me awake as much as the worry. I could not, no matter how much I thought about it, see any way to escape the trouble that lay ahead, or any way to keep my father out of it.

FOR TEN days I did not leave my father's place. Wrangel's fists had given me such a battering that I didn't feel like doing anything more than I had to. What was more, the fight showed me that I wasn't accepted in Dirken's Hole, even though I was Thomas Buel's son. They had turned on me, O'Hara and all of them, because I had whipped their man. I remembered Susan saying they would hate me like they did Hardman and Logan, and I wondered if I was being put in a class with the outlaws.

I did the chores morning and evening. During the day I worked in the garden putting away the root crops. If I had any leisure time, I spent it in the barn, sleeping in the mow if it wasn't too cold, or mending harness. The one thing I carefully avoided was being in the house alone with Susan. I could not forget what Judy O'Hara had said, that at least I should not make the situation worse. I cast around for some excuse to move to the hotel, but I could not think of one.

So the days ran on.

Whatever allure Susan had once held for me was gone. She ignored me as I ignored her. We hated each other with passion, although when my father was around, we were coolly polite. If he sensed our feelings, he gave no indication of it.

The more I watched Susan and my father when they were together, the more puzzled I became. She was a good housekeeper, apparently had worked hard all her life and didn't object to work. The house was spotless, the meals were good and on time, and she kept my father's clothes patched and ironed as neatly as my mother ever had.

It was their personal relationship that bothered me. They didn't act like man and wife, but like father and daughter, a situation that would appall a woman like Susan.

One cold afternoon in early November I was sitting on a sawhorse in the barn working on a bridle when Susan came out of the house. I was huddled over a piece of leather I was cutting, the collar of my sheepskin turned up around my neck, and I didn't know she was standing in the doorway until she spoke.

I looked up. The sky was overcast, and I supposed it was snowing on the pass. Down here the light was thin, the day a gloomy one. I stuck my knife in the other end of the sawhorse and laid the leather down, relieved to see someone, even a woman I hated and who hated me.

Every day I realized more keenly that I had been a fool to come to the Hole, that my relationship with my father would never be any closer than it had been when I'd left him more than five years ago. The thousand dollars I would receive for bringing my men in was poor pay for a winter in prison, and the Hole was a prison from which there was no escape.

Susan upended a box and sat down on it, pulling her skirt up so I could see her ankles. She was that way with men, instinctively seeking their admiration. I could hate her, but I couldn't keep from being aware of her beauty and the perfection of her body or the physical attraction that seemed to flow out of her as naturally as laughter and good humor flowed out of Judy O'Hara.

"Well?" I said.

She frowned. "What's the matter with me?"

"We don't like each other," I said. "It's that simple, isn't it?"

"But why? What have I done that's wrong?"

I rubbed a scab on my cheek, one of the marks that remained from my fight with Billy Wrangel.

"You ought to know," I said.

She gave her skirt a tug, then folded her hands on her lap and looked straight at me. "Well, I don't. If either one of us has a right to be mad, it's me, treating me the way you did at the dance."

I reached for my knife and began trimming the piece of leather. "What makes you think I didn't treat you right?"

"I suppose it was all right for you to take that O'Hara bitch out into the brush. Tom Buel's son! Tom Buel who stands for something in this country. What do you think people said about that?"

I slapped the knife back into the sawhorse, slammed the leather strap to the ground, and got up. I stood there glaring at her and fighting my temper.

38

"You're the bitch, not Judy," I said. "Only a woman with a filthy mind would say what you just said."

She laughed. "You're right down there in the same filth I'm in. I've seen it in your eyes every time you look at me."

I couldn't deny it and I didn't try. "You'd better go back to the house," I said.

"Not yet." She got up and viciously kicked the box on which she had been sitting back into the corner. "You wanted to know why I married your father. All right, I'll tell you. I wanted money and I wanted a bed partner. Tom didn't have money, but he could make it. Paul Rome does. So does Effie Castle. I wanted money to get out of here, but he won't make it. No matter what I say, he won't go after it." Her lips curled in disgust. "As for being a bed partner, I might as well be sleeping with my mother."

She whirled and stalked out. I knew I had to get out of my father's house now whether I could find a reasonable excuse or not.

Supper that night was a strained and silent meal. Afterward I sat in the front room with my father while Susan did the dishes, my father puffing on his pipe as I smoked one cigarette after another.

I watched him, the lamplight touching the side of his face that was toward me. It was thinner, his cheekbone making a sharp point under his eye. But it was not his looks so much as his spirit that seemed changed.

After Susan had gone to bed, my father asked, "How have you made a living all this time, Robert?"

The truth wouldn't do, so I said as lightly as I could, "I'm a pretty good cow hand. I never had any trouble finding a job." Then, because I was afraid that what I had done the night of the fight had made trouble for him, I added, "I don't know how many versions of my row with Wrangel have been told to you, but I want to tell you mine."

"It doesn't make any difference, Robert. If you'd rather not——"

"No, I've got to tell you."

He listened, his pipe going cold in his mouth, and when I was done, he said, "You couldn't do anything else, of course. It makes me happy to hear that Judy thinks well of me. She's a good girl, Robert. If you're looking for a wife, you would never find a better one."

"They'd set the dogs on me if I went to see her," I said. "What's O'Hara like?"

"I told you once he was the most Irish Irishman I ever saw. I meant he likes to laugh and drink and he's a fighting man. He'll dance all night and be the last one to go home usually. But there's something else, too. Billy Wrangel is a fine herder and Mike would hate to lose him. He'd have to bring in a Mexican or a Basque and he doesn't want to do either." He knocked his pipe out. "It might be he wants Judy to marry Wrangel."

"Judy won't do it," I said.

"You're probably right." He rose. "Well, I'm going to bed."

"Dad." He turned his head to look at me. "I can't just sit here like this all winter. I've got to find something to do."

"I don't know where or what it would be. Well, good night."

In the morning at breakfast he said not a single word to me. He pretended I didn't exist, and so did Susan. I didn't understand and at the moment attached no great importance to it.

After we had eaten, I saddled my horse and rode north to explore that part of the Hole I had not seen, urged by a restlessness I could not control, and driven, too, by the knowledge that I had to keep away from Susan or I would kill her. Afterward there were times when I wished I had.

8

As I rode, I discovered that the north end of the valley was much like the south half. The creek made a wide sweep to the west of the settlement, touching Dale Oren's farm, then swung back to the east and turned north not more than half a mile from my father's place. The road paralleled it for another half-mile, then swung northeast, the creek flowing northwest.

I passed one farm that looked as poverty-stricken as the others. Judging from the talk I had heard, it belonged to a man named Dick Smith. I remembered meeting him at the dance, roly-poly and pink-cheeked, with a pretty brown-eyed wife and three children. I passed the oldest one on his way to school not long after I left the settlement, riding a gray mare bareback. The other two, boys about three and five, I judged, were playing in a chip pile beside their father who was sawing wood behind the cabin.

On impulse, I turned off the road and reined up a few feet from Smith. He gave no sign that he knew I was there, but the boys saw me and stopped playing to eye me with the same curiosity I had seen many times since I had come to the Hole.

I sat my saddle in silence until Smith finished the cut and straightened, wiping his face. I said, "Howdy, Smith." He turned, apparently only then aware of my presence, stared at me a moment as if having trouble placing me, then said in a cool voice, "Howdy, Buel. I didn't hear you ride up."

He was lying. I said, "Nice day."

It wasn't a nice day at all. Judging from the dark clouds to the south, it was snowing on Chambers Pass again, and the wind that blew across the Hole held a savage bite. Winter was at hand in early November.

"Nice for what?" Smith asked sourly. "Trappers?"

I nodded. "Furs ought to be prime."

"I reckon. Well, we'll take a few, but trapping ain't what it used to be." He motioned vaguely to the northwest. "You keep riding and you'll come to the old fort. Ain't much left of it. Anything that was worth taking was took before my time."

"Army fort?"

"Hell no. Just a trading post, and a damned funny place to put one, the Hole snowed in like it always is."

He wiped sweat from his face, shivered, and turning to the log, began sawing again. I waited until he finished the cut. He had talked, but with no trace of friendliness in his voice. I had proof of what I suspected, that I was a stray in the minds of these people just as Susan was, but in a different way. Clannish, they formed a solid wall against a stranger. But I wasn't ready to give up.

When he straightened again to rest his back, I asked, "Could you use a hired hand this winter?"

"Me?" He said it as if wondering if I was hoorawing him, then apparently decided I wasn't. "Now just what would I use to pay you with? I'll be lucky if I can keep my family

41

from starving this winter. Rome didn't get in the supplies he usually does, and by March he'll have his prices higher'n a scared cat's back."

"You know of anybody who would give me a job?"

He shook his head. "Nobody but Jesse Carter and Mike O'Hara can afford to hire help, and they don't need big crews through the winter."

I shifted my weight in the saddle. "Where's O'Hara's place from here?"

He started to turn toward the log again, then swung back, swearing softly. "Why do you ask?"

"No harm finding out if he could use a man."

"I figure there is." He sat down on the log, took off his hat, wiped his face with a sleeve, and replaced his hat. "Buel, you're a fool. Or a troublemaker. Your father is respected hereabouts, and it ain't gonna make him feel any better if Billy Wrangel puts a window in your skull, which same he's gonna do if he gets a chance. Stay away from O'Hara's place."

"Where is it?"

"And another thing. Mike don't want no stranger smelling around after Judy. If Billy don't fill you full of buckshot, Mike will. Now damn it, stay away from the O'Hara ranch. We have to put up with men like you, but by God, we don't like you."

"Where is it?"

He jerked a thumb to the east. "Yonder right up next to the rim."

"Thanks," I said, and rode on.

I left the road to follow the creek, the sandstone cliffs to the north rising directly in front of me, ledge after ledge that gave the appearance of a giant staircase. I pulled up and studied the cliffs, remembering that my father had said a man could come into the valley this way but he couldn't leave. The road which had petered out to a mere trail was lost to sight from where I was, but I could see where it ran into the first ledge, and then, by using a liberal dose of imagination, I believed I could follow the path Hardman and Logan had taken into the Hole.

A good place to winter, I reflected, and a good place for a man on the dodge to get away from a posse. My years of bounty chasing had taught me a good deal about the habits

42

of such men, and spots like this were well known to all of them. They'd spend hours teaching their horses to jump six- or eight-foot precipices, but the members of the posse would be stuck at the first jump.

I laughed as I pictured the sheriff and his men who had been pursuing Hardman and Logan, sitting their saddles at the edge of the plateau utterly helpless while they could see the dust kicked up by their quarry far down the cliff. They would make the air blue with their cursing, but that was all they could do, so they'd hit the trail back to Rawlins or Rock Springs and burn up the wires trying to get some-one to go into Dirken's Hole from the south after their men, but no one would do it. The chances were Jason Harwig had got out by the skin of his teeth after shooting Link Castle. Others, both lawmen and range detectives, wanted no part of it.

This line of reasoning led me to a suspicion that was new and shocked me. I had a paper sewed inside my sheepskin which had been written and signed by Jason Harwig re-questing that I be given help by all law-abiding citizens from whom I needed help in making an arrest. I had argued with him about taking it, but Harwig beat me down, insisting I needed something to give me official status. He said more than one sheriff in what he called "the half-outlaw country" would prefer not to cooperate and would be as likely as not to throw me into jail and let my prisoners go unless I could prove I was what I said I was.

So I took the paper and sewed it inside the lining of my coat. No one upon casual inspection would find it, but Susan might have. It was possible, too, that she had found the reward dodgers offering one thousand dollars for my cap-ture. My clothes had been in my bedroom and she had been alone in the house day after day. She'd had ample time to go through them. If she had found either the paper or the reward dodgers, she could have spread the word. Perhaps it was that more than the fact that I had whipped Billy Wrangel which made an outcast of me.

I rode on, working this idea around in my head and not being quite sure whether I had stumbled onto anything or not. The way my father had acted at breakfast was so unlike him that now I began to wonder if this might be the explanation of his behavior. I tried to put it out of my mind, telling myself I was blaming Susan for everything. Still, I wasn't sure.

Near noon I came to a rectangular pile of rotten logs which I judged were ruins of the old trading post. I got down and kicked around the logs for a time, to amuse myself more than anything else. I found a few pieces of broken pottery, some pieces of metal, probably poor quality knives that were part of the fort's trading stock and now so rusty they were hardly recognizable, and a few arrow and spear heads.

The sun was noon high and still overcast when I mounted and rode on down the creek which already was getting smaller. I was hungry, but I'd get nothing to eat out here, and when I thought about what I'd have to go back to, I doubted that I'd get anything to eat in my father's house. I was in a hell of a fix and no mistake. I'd have to live in the hotel, if I lived anywhere, and I didn't have the money to pay for a winter's board and room.

I had no way, of course, to get at my money which was deposited in a Grand Junction bank. Now, with the wisdom of hindsight, I realized I should have brought several hundred dollars with me, but I couldn't foresee what I was getting into, so I had simply planned to live with my father which would cost me little or nothing.

I followed the creek down through the little cut it had dug here in the north end of the Hole, watching it get smaller and smaller and finally disappear entirely into the cracks of the sandstone. Beyond, the earth tipped up sharply, for here I was directly under the cliff, which at this point rose a sheer fifty feet above me, polished smooth by millions of years of wind erosion.

When I rode out of the cut which held the lost creek, I found myself surrounded by hundreds of rock upthrusts, carved by the wind into all kinds of shapes: obelisks, arches, grinning gargoyles, and animal figures. It was nature's graveyard, as weird and lonely a scene as I had ever looked at.

I crossed a sagebrush flat, heading in the direction that I thought would bring me to O'Hara's ranch. Off to the north, I could hear sheep, up in the broken country at the foot of the rim, and again I thought of this strange, isolated valley, divided between a sheepman and a cattleman.

Farmers were here, caught between the two; Paul Rome and Effie Castle, business people who profited from both. A little world of its own.

Ahead of me I saw a sharp ridge dotted by boulders that had fallen from the slick rock rim at the top. I saw a break and headed for it, thinking of Dick Smith's warning and discarding it. I wanted to see Judy. She had been in my mind ever since the night of the dance, and I sensed she was interested in me. As for my trouble with Billy Wrangel, the sooner it came to a head, the better. Still, I was totally unprepared for it when it did come.

I saw the twinkle of powder flame from the rim, heard the bullet whip overhead and the echoing slam of rifle fire. Old habit brought me out of the saddle in a rolling fall. I scrambled on hands and knees to the cover of a tall boulder, but even before I reached it, a man called, "Come on up, Buel. It's that God-damned Billy Wrangel, but we've got him."

For a moment I lay motionless, face down in the sagebrush. I knew the voice. I'd heard it after I'd whipped Wrangel and the crowd was hungry for my hide. It was Eli Hardman's.

9

MY BUCKSKIN labored up the steep slope, muscles straining, hoofs dislodging rocks that kicked up more rocks to make a dusty avalanche below me, and all the time I kept asking myself why Eli Hardman had interfered twice to save my life. Then the thought hit me. Maybe he hadn't interfered; maybe Billy Wrangel wasn't there at all.

If Hardman had guessed why I was in the Hole, he could have fired the shot, and blamed it on Wrangel so I would ride up to the rim. Then he and Logan would have me under their guns. They could take their time telling me what they thought of a man who was one thing when he pretended to be another, and then they could kill me. But I was out in the open now; it was too late to do anything except bull it through and hope Hardman hadn't lied.

A moment later I topped the rim, my right hand wrapped around the butt of my holstered gun. Then the tension was gone and I was weak with the sudden relief. Billy Wrangel was there, all right, his face still bearing the marks of my fists.

45

He was the ugliest, most animal-like man I had ever seen in my life. He hadn't shaved since the night of the dance, slobber was running down both sides of his mouth, and fear had taken hold of him until he was trembling. He was whimpering, "Don't kill me, Hardman. Don't kill me."

Both men were holding their guns on Wrangel. Eli Hardman was middle-aged, as stocky as Mike O'Hara. I judged the lanky man in his middle twenties would be Sam Logan. They looked at me and then at Wrangel, their faces showing the utter contempt they had for him.

"He's your meat, Buel," Hardman said, and holstered his gun. "Shoot him."

When I hesitated, Logan urged, "Go on, plug him. If you don't, he'll get you next time certain."

Wrangel stopped whimpering, but he still trembled. I suppose he thought it was no use to beg me for his life. I dismounted and shook my head at Hardman. I knew they were right, that I would not be safe as long as I stayed in the Hole and Billy Wrangel was alive. But to shoot an unarmed man, even a madman who had tried twice to kill me, was something I could not do.

"I can't beef him," I said. "Not with him standing there like that."

Hardman had an enormous black mustache that must have taken half his life to raise and covered so much of his mouth that it was impossible to recognize the expression his lips held. His eyes were light blue, and for a moment they met mine squarely, but I couldn't read the expression in them any more than I could read his mouth. Suddenly he turned his gaze to Wrangel.

"I don't reckon I could, neither," he said.

But Logan was younger and brash, and he had no patience with me. "What the hell, Buel? You'd shoot a mad dog, wouldn't you? That's what this bastard is. He'll keep trying, and chances are me'n Eli won't be around next time."

"I still can't do it," I said.

Logan motioned to Wrangel's rifle that was on the ground about ten feet from him. "Give it to him. Make him fight."

I shook my head again. I had what I thought was a better idea. I wanted to see Judy again, and I was convinced that if I killed Wrangel, I would never be welcome at the O'Hara

46

ranch, so I said, "I'm going to turn him over to O'Hara. I don't think he believed Wrangel tried to brain me with that single-tree, but maybe he'll believe this."

"He won't," Logan said in disgust, "so me'n Eli will tag along to see the fun."

Hardman picked up Wrangel's rifle and tossed it over the rim. "No, O'Hara won't believe you. I know how these people are. They'll side their own folks every time." He motioned toward a ridge to the east. "Me'n Sam were riding along there when we seen Wrangel scrooched down watching something, so we Injuned up on him and we spotted you just as he let go with that shot. We nailed him before he could get another one off. You're lucky he didn't plug you."

"I'm lucky you came along," I said. "That's the second time you've sided me, so I'm twice lucky."

He looked at me and I think he was grinning under that big mustache. "I reckon you are at that," he said. Logan brought their horses up and Hardman mounted. "Let's ride. I want to see your face when O'Hara calls you a liar."

Logan stepped into the saddle. "His face is gonna look twice as funny when O'Hara's redheaded girl gives him a cussing. That's what I want to see."

I motioned for Wrangel to get on his horse, then I swung up. He'd got over his scare, now that he knew I wasn't going to kill him. His face, dark and sullen, left no doubt in my mind that I was making a mistake. I knew what Hardman and Logan were thinking: I was soft. Well, come spring when the pass was open, they'd find out how soft I was.

Hardman and Logan led the way through the cedars to O'Hara's ranch. Wrangel rode behind them, and I followed him, my gun in my hand. He wouldn't bolt because he knew I had the gun.

Within half an hour we reached O'Hara's ranch—a number of corrals, a shed for horses, a few other outbuildings of various sizes and shapes, and a square log house with a sod roof. Mike O'Hara, reputedly one of the richest men in the Hole, lived little better than the poverty-stricken farmers along the creek.

The buildings were set against the east wall of the Hole. I could not see a flowing stream, but judging from the clumps of willows on both sides of the house, I thought there must be a number of springs that flowed out of the rocks at the base of the wall. No one was in sight.

"Well?" Hardman said, watching me closely.

"Where do you figure O'Hara is?" I asked Wrangel.

"Around," Wrangel answered.

"Where?"

"How the hell would I know?"

"Holler," I said.

He scowled, his narrow forehead knotted by deep lines under the brim of his slouch hat. He looked at my gun, then at my face, and he turned his head and bawled, "Mike."

O'Hara came striding out of the shed carrying a Winchester. He gave us no greeting of any kind. He walked straight to us, his boot heels pounding on the hard, hoof-packed yard. When he stopped, he tipped his head back, his face ugly with hostility. I couldn't help thinking it would be a hell of a fight between him and Hardman. They were built alike, short and stocky with thick arms and necks. I could sense none of the good humor that had been in O'Hara the night I'd talked to him before the dance. Just meanness, and suddenly it struck me that it would take very little to jar him into violence.

"What's the gun for, Buel?" O'Hara demanded. "Weren't you satisfied the night of the dance?"

"I was," I said, "but this plug-ugly of yours wasn't. He tried to dry-gulch me. He'd have made it if Hardman and Logan hadn't been around."

"They're by-God liars," Wrangel said harshly. "They got the drop on me and fetched me here. I didn't do nothing, Mike. Not nothing."

O'Hara stepped back so his rifle covered Hardman. My gun was on Wrangel, so I didn't think O'Hara would shoot. I said, "Go easy, mister. I'm not lying. I should have shot Wrangel. Now you can be sure of one thing. If he tries to kill me, I'll get him. I've got to stay in the Hole all winter, and I don't figure on looking over my shoulder every minute I'm here."

Mike O'Hara was not capable of reasoning beyond the one fact that Wrangel worked for him and he had to stand behind his man. He said, "You lied about who used the singletree, and you're lying now. I didn't like the idea of you walking out of the dance with Judy no more than Billy did. Let Judy alone and stay away from here. Savvy?"

I stared at him, unable to believe I had heard right. He was saying almost what Susan had said about me taking Judy into the brush, that he didn't trust his own daughter with a man when she was out of his sight.

"You're a fool, O'Hara," I said hotly. "The biggest fool——"

"Ease up, son," Hardman said. "The girl's got us looking at some buckshot. This ain't our day."

"That's right," O'Hara said. "Get out of here while you can ride."

I glanced at the house. Judy was standing in the doorway, a double-barreled shotgun in her hand. If it was loaded with buckshot, and it probably was, she could blow two of us out of our saddles at this distance, and O'Hara would get the other one. I could nail Wrangel, but that wouldn't be any help. I couldn't believe it, yet there she was, wearing a house dress with an apron tied around her waist, the wind tugging at a lock of unruly red hair that dangled across her forehead.

Without a word I holstered my gun and rode away, Hardman and Logan following. I was sick, physically sick.

Hardman and Logan came up beside me. Logan said, "It wasn't funny, Buel, seeing the look on your face. I didn't expect that of her, neither."

If a fight had started, Hardman would have been the first to go down because O'Hara had kept him covered from the time Wrangel had said he hadn't done anything. It had been close, too close, but now Hardman laughed. He said, "They're all like that, Buel. Except Effie Castle. If there's trouble, they'll stand together every damned time."

"A hell of a note," I said bitterly. "But that wasn't like Judy. I can't believe it happened."

"Blood's thicker'n water," Hardman said. "Maybe she don't like Wrangel, but O'Hara's her pappy."

We rode in silence for a time, heading across the mesa toward the settlement. Presently Logan said, "Looks like a long, hard winter. No women, and nothing to drink but Rome's rotgut."

"Chances are we'll have some excitement before spring." Hardman glanced at me as if wondering whether I was of a mind to open up. He said tentatively, "Me'n Sam are spending our vacation here in the Hole. Gets a mite tiring now and then, so we get out and take a ride. That's why we was out here. Sometimes we sit in Rome's saloon and drink his liquor and play poker, or just gab with Effie, and then by God, we've done it all. If you're on a vacation, too, you might help us entertain ourselves."

They thought they had me pegged. But I wasn't ready to declare myself yet. So I said, "Sure, I'm on a vacation."

Hardman laughed easily as if I had just confirmed his judgment of me. He said, "Bad whiskey is better'n no whiskey. Let's git along."

10

PAUL ROME'S saloon was a lean-to built against the north side of the store building. It had a front door that opened into the street and a side door that led from the saloon into the store. I had never been inside the room, partly because I seldom drank, never having acquired a taste for liquor, but mostly because of my father's attitude toward a teacher drinking. I had a vague feeling that this applied to a teacher's son, too. But today was different. I welcomed this opportunity to become friendly with Hardman and Logan.

The place looked like any saloon in a country as primitive as this. A rough pine bar ran along the store wall. Behind it a number of shelves held a variety of bottles. Three poker tables occupied the other side of the room, the green baize worn and marred by liquor stains.

Hardman sat down at a table, winked at me, and then pounded the top with his enormous fist. "Service," he bellowed. "By God, I never seen worse service."

Rome ran in from the store, the white apron tied just above the bulge of his belly. "What'll it be, gents?" he asked. Then he saw me, and his face took on the look of a man who has just had a drink of clabbered milk.

As I sat down, Hardman said out of the corner of his mouth but loud enough for me to hear, "I don't believe Rome likes you, Buel."

I hadn't seen Rome since the night of the dance. As far as I knew, he had no reason not to like me, but there was no

50

mistaking the look he gave me. Dick Smith this morning, then O'Hara, and now Rome. I said, "I don't give a damn whether he likes me or not." I nodded at him. "Beer."

"Whiskey," Logan said, and then to me, "You're making a mistake, Buel. Rome's the big cheese in this country."

"Whiskey for me." Hardman looked at me and added blandly, "Sam's right. You ought to look up to Rome and then bow down to him."

Rome brought our drinks. His face was usually very pale from inside living, but now it was as red as a freshly cut slice of beef. Hardman tipped back his chair, his pale blue eyes bright with the deviltry that was working in him.

"How much dinero you got in that safe, Rome?" Hardman asked.

"My business," Rome snapped.

"Now that ain't no way to answer a civil question," Hardman said. "Is it, Sam?"

"Hell no," Logan said affably. "You'll have to learn manners when you're talking to your betters."

Rome choked, glaring at Logan. He opened his mouth to say something, but no words came out. Just an incoherent sound, then he whirled and ran back into the store. Before he was out of the room, Hardman and Logan were laughing so hard that tears were in their eyes.

"What are you rawhiding him for?" I asked after Rome was out of the room.

Neither of them could answer for a moment, then Hardman wiped his eyes. He said, "It's fun to make him mad. It works the same way every time. He starts to give us a cussing, but he can't get a word out."

"There's the damnedest bunch of people in this valley I ever ran into," Logan said. "I don't like none of 'em but Effie Castle, and they don't like us." He scratched an ear, frowning. "But your dad now. He's another breed of dogs. Don't seem to fit. He'd be all right if it wasn't for that bitchy wife of his."

I didn't want to talk about either my father or Susan, so I asked, "Is it true Rome's got a lot of money in his safe?"

"Effie claims there's better'n twenty thousand," Hardman said. "He's got the nearest thing there is to a bank. Carter, O'Hara and Effie deposit their cash with him which saves them carrying it around or hiding it at home. They draw on it whenever they want to. Write out a check when they buy hay from the farmers, then the farmers come here for supplies and Rome honors the checks. Wouldn't surprise me none if there was more'n twenty thousand. Rome's bound to have some dinero of his own."

"Ought to be worth looking into," Logan said. "Along about the first of June."

"You know better," Hardman said harshly. "We'd have every man in the Hole on our necks." He looked at me. "Don't you get no ideas, neither. It'd ruin a good wintering place."

"Not me." I remembered what Harwig had said about someone in the Hole buying money that was too hot to spend, but when I mentioned it, Hardman shook his head.

"I don't believe it. Some of the boys get sore for one reason or another. Like if Effie trades 'em a poor horse, which she will every time she gets a chance, they holler 'bout being cheated. I never knew a case like you mentioned, though."

I drank my beer, put the glass down and rubbed the back of my neck. "Wish somebody was a barber around here," I said. "I was in too big a hurry getting here to stop for a haircut."

"I'll cut it," Logan said. "I ain't no professional barber, but I'll get you sheared."

"He don't do bad." Hardman glanced at Logan and began to laugh. "I recollect the time me'n Sam were in Cripple Creek. Right about the top of the boom. You couldn't even find a room. Well, we figured we'd better buy us a shave and a haircut, but every barber shop was packed, that being a Saturday night. We was gonna look up a couple of girls that had moved in from Leadville, and we didn't want to wait, so we walked into a barber shop, Sam first, then me. I took a look at him and began to cuss him. I calls him a mangy sheepherder and he calls me an ugly son of a bitch . . ."

Hardman was laughing so hard he couldn't talk. Logan said, "I always have to finish the story. He gets that far and he thinks it's so funny he can't wind it up. Well, we went for our guns and every man in the shop thought it was the real thing. They busted out of there like a herd of boogered steers. Two of 'em that was in the chairs had lather all over their mugs, and the one in the bathtub came boiling out with noth-

52

ing on but a towel. Damned if he didn't drop one end of it and trip on it."

"You oughta seen the barbers," Hardman said, wiping his eyes. "That was the funniest part of the whole shebang. They sure hugged the floor. One of 'em knocked the spittoon over when he fell down and got his face in the mess. I thought he'd choke hisself to death. He finally got outside and almost drowned in the horse trough."

"Did you ever get a haircut?" I asked.

"Yeah, we did," Logan answered, "but we seen it wasn't such a smart antic after all. We emptied the chairs, all right, and climbed in, but when the barbers got back to work, their hands was shaking so much it looked like we'd get our throats cut before they got the whiskers off."

"We was about as purty as a pair of butchered hogs," Hardman said, "but the girls didn't care." He stopped laughing and shook his head. "We sure had ourselves a time that night. I wish them girls was in Dirken's Hole right now."

"Gonna be a long, hard winter like I told you," Logan said.

They were silent for several minutes, both thinking, I suppose, of the women they couldn't have. Perhaps that was what brought Logan's mind to Susan. He asked, "How about that stepmother of yours? I reckon a man wouldn't have to ask her twice."

Before I could answer, Hardman broke in, "You'd have to beat her off with a club. What the hell, Sam? That's a fool question to ask a man."

"Yeah, it was," Logan agreed. "I apologize, Buel."

"Sure," I said, thinking how a man's honor worked. Here were two outlaws who would hold up a train or probably kill a man without any great provocation, but taking an honest man's wife was completely out of the question. Then, because they were friendly men who understood my problem, or maybe because the problem had burdened me right from the first moment I had seen Susan in my father's kitchen, I said, "I've got to get out of my dad's house."

"Why don't you move over to the hotel?" Hardman asked. "Effie's a right good cook."

"I'm broke," I told him. "I didn't have much time when

53

I got over the pass. I haven't got twenty dollars in my pocket, and that won't pay for a winter's board and room."

Logan took his drink and set the glass down. He looked at Hardman but said nothing. I soon learned that was the way they operated and it was the reason their partnership was nearly perfect. Hardman was the older with mature judgment, Logan was the brash one who had made enough mistakes to learn that the smart thing to do was to let Hardman take the lead.

"Well now, Buel," Hardman said, "let's think on this awhile. Ain't much work in the Hole during the winter. If I kicked Rome in the belly, he'd give you a job, but you wouldn't like it."

"You'd be in the fire instead of the frying pan," Logan grunted.

Hardman downed his drink and carefully set the glass in the middle of the table. He brushed one side of his mustache with the blunt ends of the fingers of his right hand, did the same with the other side, then he said thoughtfully, "Now Effie might give you a job just for your bed and grub. Let's go ask her."

I didn't think there was a ghost of a show, but I was in a position where I'd grab at anything. We left the saloon, and mounting, rode around the hotel to the barn. It was dusk, and as we cleared the corner of the hotel, we saw a lighted lantern hanging above the door.

"She's cleaning out the barn," Logan said in disgust. "Supper's gonna be late again, and we didn't eat no dinner."

"You can't blame her," Hardman said, "doing a man's work and hers, too. I figure you've got a job, Buel."

We dismounted, Hardman and Logan leading their horses into the barn. I stayed outside, getting a good look at Effie, who straightened up and leaned on the handle of her pitchfork. If I had drawn a picture of Effie Castle based on what I had heard of her, I would not have been far wrong.

She was close to sixty, big and rawboned with hair as black as shoe polish. I had a hunch that was exactly what she used on her hair, and if she ever got caught in a rain storm, it would come streaking down her face. She had a fat nose and a strong chin, and a whiskery upper lip that looked as if she had a smudge of dirt under her nose that wouldn't wash off.

"Better get inside and start cooking our supper, Effie," Hardman said. "I'm hungry enough to eat a horse."

"That's what you're gonna get," Effie said. "Horse steak."

"We don't want to eat no horse," Logan said. "We've already paid for our meals. You get to work."

Effie snorted. "Well, by God, if you ain't the good ones to talk. If you wasn't such lazy bastards, you'd do this work and I could get into the kitchen when it's time. Now go soak your head in the horse trough. You'll get supper when I cook it and no sooner."

Hardman called, "Come in here, Buel."

I led my buckskin into the barn. Effie spun around as Hardman said, "Effie, this here is Bob Buel, the school teacher's son. Reckon you've seen him."

"Seen him and heard of him." Effie offered a calloused hand and I shook it. "Right happy to meet the gent that whipped Billy Wrangel."

"I'm looking for a job," I said. "Just for my board and room. Taking care of your stock and doing work like you're doing and——"

"Hold on, mister, hold on." Effie turned to look at Hardman, who was laughing. "You son of a bitch, this is a put-up job if I ever seen one. I oughta use my pitchfork and poke a few extra holes in your——"

"Cool down, Effie," Logan said. "This here is a bonny fide proposition. We're just trying to fix it so you'll get our suppers on time."

Effie handed the fork to me. "Finish up. Put your horse in the back stall. I'll go get supper started." She glared at Hardman. "And by God, I hope it chokes you."

Hardman was still laughing when she stalked out. He said, "You see, Buel? All you had to do was ask."

I took care of my horse, then started filling the wheelbarrow. I wasn't fooled. Not a little bit. Effie knew a lot more about Eli Hardman and Sam Logan than I did. I think she was afraid of them, but whether she was or not, I was sure of one thing. It was their asking, not mine, that got me the job.

11

I TOOK to Effie Castle right from the start. There was no put-on about her. Her black, black hair was the only vanity she seemed to have. She was careless about her clothes, but she was clean and she kept the hotel clean. Her face was wrinkled and as leathery brown as Eli Hardman's, but I'm sure it didn't bother her at all. Her salty speech was filled with profanities and obscenities, and she made no apology. You liked her the way she was or you didn't, and she pretended she didn't much care.

When I came in from the barn that first night, I washed on the back porch and went into the kitchen. She stood at the big range frying meat. When she heard me, she yelled at Hardman and Logan, who were in the front of the house, "Come and git it or I'll throw it to the dogs."

She turned to look at me as if she dared me to talk out of turn. "Sit down, Bob. I ain't no fancy cook. You might as well find that out now, but I always put enough victuals on the table to fill a gut the size of yourn. You don't have to like my grub, but you'd better be by-God sure you don't say so."

I didn't, either. Compared to most of the places where I had eaten during the last five years, her food was exceptionally good. She put meat, beans, potatoes, biscuits, hot black coffee and apple pie on the table. I hadn't had dinner. Hardman and Logan hadn't, either. We ate wolfishly, and when we were finally satisfied, Effie looked sorrowfully at the empty dishes and shook her head.

"Reckon I'll have to start all over again tomorrow." She got up, and walking to a shelf on the wall, lifted the lid from a brown, round-bellied crock, took out a cigar, and returned to her chair at the table. "Well, I never in all my born days seen three hogs in human form afore. If I hadn't watched that grub disappear with my own eyes, I wouldn't have believed it."

"We're paying you two prices for the chance to eat it," Hardman said, "and if I know you, Buel's gonna get his tail worked off. I'll bet you never came out short on a deal in your life."

Effie lighted her cigar and sat back in her chair, an expression of absolute contentment on her face. "I figure on working him, but as far as you two varmints go, I'm losing money every time you pull your bellies up to my table."

Hardman snorted his derision. "Like hell you are." He got up. "Sam, let's mosey over to the saloon and hooraw old Rome some more."

"What about this time?" Logan asked.

"Why, we might work on his prices." Hardman grinned. "That makes him madder'n anything else."

"Wouldn't surprise me none if he ordered that early storm so he could take advantage of it, he'll do it, too," Effie said.

"Chances are he didn't want them three wagons of supplies to get in," Hardman said. "Probably told his drivers to sit down and wait for the snow."

"Maybe he never even started 'em," Logan said. "Just claimed he did."

Effie slapped the table and laughed. "I'll bet that's what happened, but nobody's gonna blame the stinker. They'll come around begging for credit and he won't give 'em none, and they still won't get mad at him. That's what gravels me."

"Why won't they?" I asked.

"I dunno. I reckon it's just that he's lived here in the Hole for twenty years. His dad had the store afore he did, and the old man got a reputation for being honest. Paul inherited it along with the store. Besides, Jesse Carter and Mike O'Hara keep their money in his safe, so everybody figures he's all right or Jesse and Mike wouldn't trust him. That gravels me, too. Anything Jesse and Mike says goes."

"You keep your money there," Hardman said.

She pulled on her cigar, glaring at Hardman. "What if I do? Safer over there than here."

"Maybe," Hardman said. "Maybe not." He jerked his head at Logan. "Come on, Sam."

After they left, Effie scratched her fat nose. "Along about the first of June the snow will go off the pass and them two bastards will go loping out of here. Wouldn't surprise me none if they cleaned Paul out."

"I don't think so," I said. "They might want to winter here again some day."

57

"Yeah, I guess you're right. We've had lots of owlhooters who wintered in the Hole, or just rode through in the summer, and none of 'em ever got out of line. We don't like 'em, but they're a hell of a lot more man than the exterminators the cattlemen's association sends in here."

I caught my breath. What she had just said was a tip-off to how I'd stand if they ever found out why I was here. I tried to sound casual when I asked, "Any of them ever show up?"

She fingered the ash from her cigar, her face bitter. "A varmint named Harwig shot my boy Link in the back. If I ever get a chance at the son of a bitch, I'll cut his heart out and eat it."

Seeing the hatred in her face, I believed she'd do exactly what she said. A prickle ran along my spine. If she knew Harwig had sent me here, I'd be dead meat. I rose. "I've got to get my things from Dad's place."

"Sit down." She waved the cigar at me. "This is the one time of day when I like to sit and gab. Just long enough to smoke one cigar." I dropped back into the chair, reluctant to stay, but deciding that since this was the first night, I'd better please her.

Effie studied the glowing tip of her cigar. "I sure hate prying folks who gossip. Like Dale Oren's wife and that dried-up slut Jesse Carter found in Denver and married." She glanced at me, and added, "Hell, I don't need to pry. I know Susan, so it ain't no secret why you're moving into the hotel."

I rolled and lighted a cigarette, thinking there was no need for me to say anything. The silence ran on for a full minute, Effie wanting me to talk about it, but I wouldn't. Finally I asked, "How did Dad come to marry her?"

"Everybody wonders that," she answered. "Now I want to ask you a question. What kind of woman was your mother?"

I said, "My mother was kind and gentle. I don't remember ever hearing her speak a hard word to Dad."

"That's the kind of woman he needs," Effie said. "He's a strange and a good man. That damned Susan is killing him by inches. You see, almost all of us who live here came twenty years ago or so and settled down, or we were born and raised here and don't know nothing else. I don't like most of 'em and

58

they don't like me, but they eat their meals in the hotel when they come to the store on Saturdays and we get along 'cause we have to. I don't think any of 'em likes anybody else much. We've just lived too close together for too long. If a stranger moves in, which ain't often, he gets the cold shoulder. But now take your dad. He's the only man I can remember who was made welcome. Everybody likes him except Billy Wrangel, who don't like nobody but Mike and Judy."

"You still haven't said why he married Susan."

"Well, I just ain't sure. He used to come here for his suppers. I never charged him more'n two bits a meal 'cause he was a finicky eater. I guess he was just lonesome, living by himself the way he done. Maybe it was being alone so much that made him take up with Susan. And when Susan gets a notion to honey up to you, she can make you think black's white. If you're a trusting soul like Tom is, why, it's all the easier."

"But why would she marry him?"

"That's as plain as the big nose on my face, a lot plainer than why he married her. Susie's always wanted to be respectable. Nothing unusual about that. Most women are the same way. I'm not. I'm just a maverick."

I got up. "I've got to get over there," I said.

I walked out of the kitchen into the darkness, leaving her gripping the butt of her cigar between her teeth.

My father was sitting beside the stove, his pipe in his hands. Susan stood against the wall, frowning. My father rose and looked briefly at me. I had never seen his face quite like this, his mouth a tight, bitter line, his eyes filled with haunting misery. Without a word he whirled and stalked into his bedroom and shut the door.

I started toward the bedroom, but Susan stepped in front of me. "Do you have to be kicked in the face to take a hint?" she asked in a low tone so my father couldn't hear. "You're not welcome here any more. Do I have to write it out in big red letters?"

I said, "I'm moving into the hotel."

I went into the room I had occupied from the time I had come to the Hole. It took only a minute or two to gather my things and tie my bedroll, and all the time I was cursing myself for ever coming to Dirken's Hole.

I left the bedroom and had almost reached the front door when she said, "Bob." When I turned, she walked toward me, a warm smile on her full lips. "Bob, I could fix it so you wouldn't have to go."

I didn't want to talk to her. I turned toward the door and she grabbed my coat. "Bob, don't you understand? You never noticed me. I was like dirt under your feet. I had to do something to make you——"

"Are you Potiphar's wife?" I asked.

"Pot . . ." She stared at me blankly. "What are you talking about?"

"There was a man who lived in Egypt," I said. "He made the mistake of leaving his coat in Potiphar's wife's room. I'll keep mine on."

I went out, leaving her standing there.

12

THROUGH THE following weeks I saw to it that Effie had no cause to find fault with my work. I got up before she did, built a fire and put the teakettle on the stove, went outside and fed and milked her cows, and chopped wood until she called breakfast.

During the day I took care of her horses, cleaned out the barn, mended the harness, which was badly in need of repair, worked on the corrals and hauled hay from Dale Oren's or Dick Smith's farm. On Saturdays, when Jesse Carter and his wife and most of the Skull crew had dinner in the hotel along with a few farmers like Oren who felt like splurging, I washed dishes.

Hardman said testily a man was a fool for working any harder than he had to. Logan needled me about making up to Effie and being the cook's pet. As far as Effie was concerned, she said she hadn't had it so easy since Link got plugged, and she allowed she'd have time for a cigar after dinner as well as one after supper.

But work was no virtue on my part. I had to do it. I couldn't sleep at night unless I was dead-tired. If I had been a drinking man, I would have got drunk and stayed drunk, but I had learned a long time ago that a man who lived by the gun had no business drinking. What I needed was a fight, a brutal, punishing fight like the one I'd had with Billy Wrangel the night of the dance, but Wrangel stayed away from the settlement and there was no one else I wanted to fight.

If I had any leisure time, I spent it in the saloon with Hardman and Logan, listening to them needle Rome. Or playing poker with them in their hotel room. Or just sitting at the table after supper talking to Effie while she smoked her cigar.

I had been around outlaws before, but never on a friendly basis. The outlaws I had known were in jail and I was their jailer, or I was bringing them to jail and therefore was their enemy. I hated them and they hated me, and any good qualities they had escaped me.

Now, and I had to admit this to myself, I had never been with men who were easier to get along with than Hardman and Logan. If I'd had to choose between being with them or Jason Harwig, the decision would have been no problem. By any standards I could apply, they were good human beings. The fact that they had held up and robbed a train of fifty thousand dollars seemed a distant and impersonal act.

Then I would start thinking about how they had saved my life on two occasions and how I was duty-bound to take them to jail as soon as the pass opened, and my thinking stopped. All I knew was that I hated myself, and I was in a jackpot I didn't know how to get out of.

Once I went to the schoolhouse after four to talk to my father when he would be alone. I met him just as he was leaving. He shut the door and looked at me, a bitter, condemning man. Before I could say a word, he said, "I don't want to talk to you, Robert. I don't even want to see you again. I hope you will leave the Hole as soon as the pass is open. Until it is, just stay away from me."

"I've got a right to know why you say that," I said. "What have I done?"

Tears ran down his cheeks and the corners of his mouth began to quiver. He swallowed twice before he could say, "Robert, I've been in hell since you've been here. Must you pour salt into the wound you've made?"

"What have I done?" I asked again.

"By God, you know. Don't ask me to repeat it."

He walked away. I had never heard him swear before.

I had tried to make up with him, I told myself, and I would not try again. He had been plain. "Stay away from me," he had said, and that's exactly what I would do. But there was one other thing I must do, and somehow I had a vague hope it would make me feel better. I had to visit my mother's grave.

I went on a Sunday in early December, a warm day for that time of year. For once it was not snowing on the pass. The mountains rolled up ahead of me in a rounded, white mass, but I was in no mood to appreciate beauty.

Five miles from the settlement I was in snow. It gradually deepened until my buckskin had hard going by the time I reached the place where we had camped more than five years ago and my mother had died. Suddenly I realized how futile this ride was. I could not, no matter how hard I tried, find the grave under its deep covering of snow.

The creek, very low, made almost no sound, its edges covered by a lacework of ice. I stayed there a long time, remembering how my mother loved the sound of a mountain stream and the whisper of the aspen leaves. But I could not recover the feeling that had been in me as my mother had talked to me just before she died. It had happened too long ago.

I found it impossible to talk to anyone about my troubles, even Effie, but I think she understood, partially at least, what was wrong with me. She would have been the last to admit she had any tender feelings, but in spite of her efforts to disguise it, she had a big heart that sometimes got the best of her.

Effie knew what had happened at the O'Hara ranch the day I turned Wrangel over to O'Hara, and she knew what Judy had done. I didn't go back to the O'Hara ranch, and Judy didn't come to the settlement, so Effie hit on a solution in a sly way that fooled me completely because I didn't expect her to resort to trickery.

One Monday morning about a week before Christmas Effie said in an offhand way, "Bob, I want you to run an errand for me. I guess you don't have no pressing work."

"No, nothing pressing," I said.

She glanced out of the window. The sky was dark and

forbidding and she shook her head gloomily. "I dunno. May snow afore night. I kind o' hope it does. We ain't had a white Christmas since Link was a boy. I disremember just how long ago it was."

I should have seen through it then, the way she was taking the long way around, but I didn't. I asked, "What do you want me to do?"

"I want you to ride over to Dick Smith's place. I owe him for two loads of hay and with Christmas coming on, he might need the money."

Dick Smith had eaten dinner right here the previous Saturday and she could have paid him then. More than that, she owed Dale Oren for five loads of hay and Christmas was just as close for the Orens as it was for the Smiths. But Effie got peculiar notions at times, so I didn't argue. She wrote out the check and I saddled up and headed for the Smith place.

I got there just a little before noon. Smith wasn't in sight, so I knocked on the door, thinking he'd gone inside for dinner. When Mrs. Smith opened the door, she fell all over herself making me welcome.

"Come in, Mr. Buel," she cried. "Come in. It's a cold day to take a ride. You must be chilled to the bone."

I stepped in and she closed the door. Then I caught on. Judy was on the floor studying a dress pattern, her mouth full of pins. She looked up at me, trying to smile and say something, but all she did was sputter.

"Judy, take those pins out of your mouth," Mrs. Smith said.

I stood leaning against the door, my sheepskin buttoned under my chin, my hat in my hand. I suppose I got red in the face. There was no one I wanted to see more than Judy, but I knew now that Effie had been playing Cupid, conniving with Mrs. Smith, and it embarrassed me.

Judy took the pins out of her mouth. She laughed. "I heard of a woman in Rock Springs who swallowed some pins and got a perforated stomach."

Mrs. Smith was horrified. "I wouldn't know what to do for a perforated stomach. Oh, Mr. Buel, let me have your hat. Take off your coat. It's warm here in the house."

She was like a mother hen with a hawk in the sky. I said, "I came to see your husband."

"He isn't here right now. You just sit down and talk to Judy and I'll get dinner on the table."

Dress goods and pieces of a pattern were scattered all around Judy on the rag rug. I knew what had happened. Mrs. Smith had told Effie that Judy was coming over to help her with a dress and they'd schemed up this plan for getting us together. That might be fun for Effie, but I had to know how Judy felt. She was sitting with her chin on her knees, her arms around her legs, smiling as if she had figured out what had happened and we might as well enjoy the joke together.

"This is the first time I've seen you since you were looking at me over a double-barreled shotgun," I said.

"Why, Mr. Buel, she can't hit the broad side of a barn," Mrs. Smith said.

The smile left Judy's lips. "Don't lie to him, Lydia. I'm a good shot."

"You wouldn't have to be with buckshot at that distance," I said.

"No, I wouldn't," Judy admitted. "But I'm surprised at you, Bob. I thought you'd understand what I did and why I did it."

"I understand what a load of buckshot will do," I said.

"Then you're not as smart as I thought you were," she said. "I gave you and Dad a way out. When two stiff-necked men like you get together with guns in their hands, somebody is going to get hurt and I didn't want it to be either one of you."

"What about Billy Wrangel?"

"As far as I'm concerned, it's open season on him any time you have a chance," she said tartly. "But don't bring him home again. You should have known what Dad would do."

I should have, of course. If I had been in Mike O'Hara's place, I would have done the same thing. I said, "I guess I'm not very smart. The truth was I wanted to see you again."

"I take that kindly," she said. "I'd like to see you again. I'll be at the schoolhouse Friday night for the box supper."

I hadn't intended going because of my father, but I couldn't

64

say no to her. Not after she had opened the door to me. "I'll be on hand," I said. "What will your box look like?"

Judy laughed. "You know I can't tell you that. It's unethical."

"Oh, fiddledeedee," Mrs. Smith snorted. "Just for once I'd like to see you eat with someone you can stand instead of Paul Rome or Bud Stivers." She spread her hands to show me how big the box was. "I can tell you what it'll look like because I'm going to help her make it. It'll be that high and so wide and it'll have a big red bow on top and a little doll tied into the bow with a blue bonnet and a red dress."

For once Judy was embarrassed. "Lydia, what will he think with you——"

"I think I'll get a good supper." I handed Mrs. Smith the check. "Effie sent that over."

"You'll stay for dinner, won't you?"

"No, I'm starting to store up space for Friday night," I said. "What's going to be in the box, fried chicken?"

"You like fried chicken?"

"You bet I do."

"Then it'll be fried chicken. Judy's coming over Friday to help me with my dress and we'll fix the boxes together. And I'll bake a three-layer cake with whipped cream. It's Dick's favorite."

"Lydia, I declare if I ever saw you——" Judy began.

"So long," I said, and went out.

I felt better than I had for weeks as I rode back to the hotel. I had a hunch that Judy wasn't as opposed to Mrs. Smith's and Effie's matchmaking as she let on. Like any girl, she didn't want to appear eager, and I didn't want her to be. Our problem wasn't going to be with each other. Judy's trouble would be with her father and mine would be with Billy Wrangel.

When I got back to the hotel, I jumped on Effie for being underhanded and not telling me Judy was going to be at Smith's place. She stuck out her lower lip at me the way she did when she got on the defensive about anything. "I done you a favor and don't you forget it. Just one thing. Billy Wrangel ain't gonna like you eating with Judy no better'n he liked you taking her for a walk the night of the dance. So look out."

65

Effie opened the oven to see if her cake was done, and then very carefully closed the door. She sighed. "You know, Bob," she said, "all the trouble in the world is caused by greedy, proudful people, but there ain't no trouble a few good funerals won't solve."

My funeral might be among them, I thought, if some of the people in the Hole had their way.

13

EFFIE PARTIALLY had her wish granted for a white Christmas. We had a good six inches of snow the Monday afternoon I returned from Dick Smith's place, but the middle of the week turned off warm and most of the snow melted. Thursday and Friday were both cold. I don't think it went above freezing either day, so there was still snow on the ground on the north sides of the buildings, and the ground was treacherous even in the sun because the snow had melted and then frozen. I fell several times walking between the hotel and the barn, and between the barn and the corrals.

Hardman and Logan saw me go down once. It was typical of their sense of humor that they would think my fall was funny and they laughed until they cried. They were both that way when a joke or something struck them just right. At first their extravagant sense of humor puzzled me, but after I'd been around them awhile, I decided they would have gone crazy if they hadn't had some way to blow off steam. I gathered from hints they had dropped here and there that Logan had been an outlaw since he was a kid and Hardman for at least twenty years and had spent one term in the pen at Deer Lodge. But whether my notion was right or not, I was sure I had never met two men who enjoyed laughter as they did.

Within an hour it was my turn to laugh. Logan took a header between the hotel and the barn and it was a beauty. Both feet went out from under him at the same time and for an instant his entire body was in the air, his arms and legs flapping wildly so that for a second he resembled a giant, four-winged bird. He came down hard and for a time lay on his back, his breath jarred out of him.

I saw it from the barn door and Effie from the back porch

66

of the hotel. Hardman was a step behind Logan. We all laughed, but to Logan there was nothing funny about it just as I had not thought it was funny when I fell. He got up and started for me, shouting, "You damned bastard, you'd laugh if I killed myself."

I thought I had a fight on my hands, and I would have if Hardman hadn't caught him and jerking him around, slapped him on the cheek. "Come on, Sam," Hardman said. "You're a hell of a sport, now ain't you?"

Logan stopped, so furious he was panting for breath. Effie came sailing across the yard making noises like an excited Plymouth Rock hen. She got Logan by the arm and shook him. "Listen here, bucko. You start a fight with Bob and I'll throw you out head over teakettle. You'll be spending the winter in a cave. Savvy?"

Logan's rage left as fast as it had hit him. "I savvy, all right. I sure wouldn't want to miss your cooking." He winked at me. "Sorry, Bob. I guess I did look a mite funny at that."

"Funny," Effie snorted. "You looked downright ridiculous." She stomped back to the hotel. We watched her, all of us expecting her to slip. I wondered how she'd take it if we laughed at her, but she made it safely and slammed the back door as she went into the house.

Logan grinned weakly. "Well, by God, there goes a woman. She's more man than the three of us put together."

Hardman nodded. "When you got her for a friend, you got a good one." He was right, so right that I felt better than I had for weeks.

My father let school out early Friday so the children could get home and clean up for the party. All of them came in carts or buggies, or rode horses. Several of the boys took a short cut by riding between the hotel and the barn, and I heard Dale Oren's boy say, "What's the matter with old man Buel?" And Dick Smith's eight-year-old said, "I dunno, but he didn't have no cause to whop me. I'm sure gonna tell my Dad." He was sniffling as he said it. There was more grumbling as they rode on, but that was all I heard.

I brooded over it as I finished my chores. As far as I knew, my father had never had any school trouble, and I had never known him to whip a child, at least a small one like the Smith boy.

I finished the chores early because I wanted to shave before it was time to go to the schoolhouse. When I went into the kitchen with the milk, I found Effie holding a bowl on her lap and beating some kind of batter. She sat in front of the range with the oven door open, her big legs stretched toward the stove, her skirt hoisted up almost to her knees. As soon as I came in, she said, "Better shave, Bob."

"I'm going to," I said, and put the milk down and went upstairs to my room for my shaving gear.

When I came back down, I saw that Effie had hung a mirror beside the bracket lamp, for it was dusk outside, too dark to shave without a light. She had poured a wash pan of hot water and set it on the table a few feet from the mirror.

"I washed and ironed your best shirt," she said. "It ain't in very good shape. You've got to buy some new duds if you're gonna spark Judy."

"I aim to," I said, "but I've been putting it off. I'm just about broke."

"I've been thinking," she said. "You've been working real good. I figured I'd pay you a little cash. Say, ten dollars a month."

"That wasn't the deal," I said.

"Don't argue with me," she cried. "I got a right to change my mind. Here." She laid three five-dollar gold pieces on the table. "Call it a Christmas present if you want to."

"Thanks," I said, and put the money in my pocket. I was glad to get it. I needed clothes, all right, but the immediate need was money to buy Judy's basket, and I had a feeling that Mike O'Hara would have somebody try to outbid me just to keep me from eating with Judy.

Because I couldn't get out of my mind what I had heard the boys say, I told Effie about it, and how I'd tried to talk to my father one afternoon at the schoolhouse and he'd told me to stay away from him.

"It isn't like him," I said. "He's always been fair, and he acted glad to see me when I first got here."

"You know what happened as well as I do," Effie said. "Susan's poisoned him with her lies. If I know Tom, he's the kind who thinks he's got to trust his wife even if it means turning against his son. Maybe she said you're an outlaw. Or

68

that you propositioned her. If you had, everything would be lovey-dovey."

"Yeah, if we could have fooled him."

"It'd be easy. You can always fool people who trust you." She pounded the table with a fist. "I tell you, Bob, we're all a little crazy and we've all got some wickedness in us. Like that floozy Jesse Carter married. Got all a woman could ask for on Skull, but she makes up gossip about everybody in the Hole while the talk is she's sleeping with half the Skull crew. Mostly Bud Stivers, I guess. But she ain't all bad. Take the time Dale Oren's baby got the croup and Mrs. Oren was sick in bed. Mrs. Carter moved in and took care of things. But Susie, she's all bad."

I said, "She's a good housekeeper."

"Yeah, you've gotta give the devil her due," Effie admitted grudgingly. "She worked when she was here. That's a fact. But it's nothing to balance off the bad that's in her. I think she killed Link. If I could prove it, I'd slit her throat. By God, I would."

"What are you talking about?" I asked. "I thought Harwig did it."

Effie took a long breath and blew it out in a great gust. "I'd better go back a piece. You see, Link found her in Rock Springs when she was sixteen. They claimed she was a waitress in a restaurant, but I always figured he got her out of a house. Anyhow, Link wasn't no great catch. He told some lies about owning a big spread, so she married him. When he got her here, she found out we just had a little old hotel and not much stock and she was in for a lot of hard work. She ding-donged him about taking her out of here, but he didn't have no money. Finally, and I blame her for it, he teamed up with some ridge runners and left the Hole. He was back in a week with a bullet-busted left arm. He wouldn't talk about it. Not to me. Maybe he did to Susie. Anyhow, Harwig showed up in a couple of weeks and plugged Link. I think she wrote to Harwig telling him where Link was, hoping he'd pay for the information."

I shook my head, still not believing she had turned Link in. "Link was a young man. He must have been a better husband than Dad."

"Naw, he wasn't worth shucks as a husband. Besides, him

69

and me aren't respectable. I told you that. Didn't bother us. We just wouldn't squat down in front of Jesse Carter or Mike O'Hara or Paul Rome and lick their boots, and they're the ones that count in this country. Well, Tom's respectable if he ain't nothing else and it could be she had an eye on him while Link was still alive."

Effie was wound up and would have talked more if Hardman and Logan hadn't come in, Logan sniffing and shaking his head. "I can't smell no supper, Effie. What's the matter with you, gone lazy?"

"No, I ain't lazy," she snapped. "You're gonna buy your supper at the schoolhouse. Get cleaned up, both of you."

"You know we keep out of these shindigs," Hardman objected. "These people hate us and we don't like them."

"Tonight you're going." Effie got up. "If you don't buy a basket, come back and I'll fix you a meal that'll make you pop. Meanwhile Bob here needs a little help."

Hardman and Logan looked at each other questioningly, then Hardman said, "I don't trust you, Effie. On a deal like this, you're as tricky as a white-eyed cayuse."

"You bet I am," she said. "Now I'll tell you what to do. There'll be a box come up about so big." She measured with her hands. "All done up purty with white paper and red ribbon. Everybody's gonna think it's Judy's, but it's Mrs. Smith's. O'Hara'll have somebody primed to bid on it. Might be Bud Stivers. Or Paul Rome. Bob will go up to five dollars and quit. Then one of you boys jump in and run it up. Make 'em pay through their damned noses."

Effie had been talking so fast she ran out of breath. Hardman and Logan considered it a minute, then they laughed and Hardman said, "Sure, we wouldn't miss a deal like that, but how's Bob coming off?"

"If I've got it figured right, Judy's basket will come up right after Mrs. Smith's. Bob oughta get it for three, four dollars. The girl's name is always on the inside, so it'll take whoever gets Mrs. Smith's a while to find out it ain't Judy's. By that time Bob's already bought Judy's. Now if it don't work that way, you back Bob for all you've got in them saddlebags upstairs. He's just naturally got to get Judy's."

"He'll get it," Hardman said.

"Let's whack our whiskers off, Eli," Logan said. "Looks like a fine large evening."

I went upstairs and put on my clean shirt and another pair of pants. I slipped my gun under my waistband. Guns weren't allowed, but with Billy Wrangel there, it would be suicide to go without it. If I kept my coat buttoned, no one would see it.

As I went downstairs, I heard rigs bumping along the frozen road in front of the hotel. Crowds gathered early in Dirken's Hole. I put on my coat, thinking of what lay ahead. There would be trouble with Billy Wrangel sooner or later. It was written in the book. Maybe tonight was as good a time as any.

14

I WALKED to the schoolhouse with Hardman and Logan, the thin ice on the shallow puddles in the road crackling under our feet. The sky was clear, the stars glittering like hoarfrost in early-morning sunshine. There was no moon, so the light was very thin. We walked slowly, putting our feet down gingerly. I remembered the fall I had taken earlier that day, and Logan, I suppose, was remembering his, but Hardman seemed to have his mind on something else.

The front door of the schoolhouse was closed because of the cold, but the windows were bright with lamp light that fell in long yellow fingers on the frozen ground. Even with the windows and door closed, we could hear the woman chatter and the excited giggles of children.

"Sounds like the inside of a lonesome henhouse that ain't got a rooster," Hardman said sourly.

"It's Christmas," Logan said.

He was thinking, I was sure, of his own boyhood, and so was I. The night was the same as so many other nights I could remember at Christmas, bright and starry-eyed and cold with the ground frozen hard under foot, but the magic of childhood could never quite be brought back. Just for a moment I almost had it, and I imagined I could see my mother's face framed at one of the windows, looking out to discover if anyone was coming and saying worriedly as she always did that we just couldn't get the decorating done before the crowd came, but we never failed. Then this gossamer, transient picture was gone, and I thought of Susan trying to fill my mother's place and completely failing, and the last poignant memory was gone.

We joined a ring of men that had formed along the east side of the schoolhouse. Mike O'Hara produced a jug from his rig and started it around. He made his own liquor, and Effie insisted that most of Rome's stock came from O'Hara's still. Bud Stivers, Carter's foreman, took a long swig and said, "That hits the spot, Mike," and passed the jug to me. Suddenly recognizing me, he hesitated, then reluctantly let it go.

I took a drink because it was something I had to do, and passed the jug on to Logan, trying to keep from choking and not quite succeeding. It was pure lightning and how anyone could enjoy drinking the stuff was beyond me. But Logan did and passed the jug on to Hardman. A moment later my father stepped out of the schoolhouse and said, "Will you come in, gentlemen? We are ready to start the program."

I was one of the first through the door and so was able to take and hold a position in a corner with my back to the wall. All the men had to stand because the seats were filled with women and children. My father was in the front of the room waiting for the crowd to quiet down, tall and white-haired and, to me, ominously frail. Susan stood beside the manger almost under the star, her dark eyes snapping with the excitement of the moment. She was wearing a lavender and cream satin skirt with a frilled, high-collared lace blouse, and a black beaded cape around her shoulders. For this moment at least she had achieved respectability, and if it was as important to her as Effie thought, she must be happy.

I searched for Judy, but it took me a moment to locate her, sitting in one of the front seats with Lydia Smith. Judy was wearing a blue velvet dress that was attractive enough, but it was her red hair I particularly noticed, pinned into a chignon that was bright with diadem combs. She was lovely, I thought, far lovelier than any other woman in the room, even Susan standing up in front for everyone to admire just as they admired the beautifully decorated Christmas tree.

So intently was my attention fixed upon Judy that I missed my father's opening remarks.

He stepped aside to stand with Susan. The play began, first

with two little girls, one portraying Mary and the other the angel. I was astonished when I saw the angel. My mother had never made as gorgeous a robe or wings as large and shining as these. Susan had outdone herself, but as Effie had said caustically, "You have to give the devil her due."

The girls went through their parts as if they enjoyed what they were doing; the boys sullenly mumbled their lines so it was hard to hear them. That was the way it always was.

I looked at the row of men: Jesse Carter and Bud Stivers and the rest of the Skull crew, Dale Oren and Dick Smith and the other farmers, Mike O'Hara, a little flushed with his own whiskey and Billy Wrangel with his low forehead and dangling arms, and Paul Rome with his little pot belly and white skin and soft hands.

They were strong men, all but Rome, men capable of violence and familiar with it, men who would have scoffed at any hint of softness or tenderness, yet now they stood without sound or motion, their faces showing how deeply their feelings were stirred. Only Eli Hardman seemed untouched.

When the play was finished, Susan announced we would sing a few carols. She had a fine soprano voice and she set the pitch without using a tuning fork. She even had the men singing, Jesse Carter in his booming bass and Mike O'Hara in his tenor. Even Billy Wrangel tried although the noise he made was terrifying.

When Susan stepped back, my father took her place. He said, "As has been our custom, we have a basket social following the Christmas program. Our ladies have come prepared to feed you gentlemen. The only difficulty is you must pay for your supper. The money goes to the school library fund which will be used to buy books. They will arrive in time to be placed on our shelves for the opening of the fall term. Now let me introduce our genial auctioneer, Mr. Jesse Carter."

The spell was broken, the magic gone for another year. The men began to talk as Carter shoved his great body up the narrow aisle, the women chattered, the children broke loose into a combination of giggles, feet shuffling, shrieks and other noises that defied identification.

Hardman poked me in the ribs. He said out of the corner of his mouth, "Take a look at Wrangel."

I looked, and quickly glanced away. His eyes were pinned

73

on me, hot with the wild hatred he had for me. He would do something before the evening was over, I thought, but I doubted that he would bid against me. He wasn't smart enough. But O'Hara, I was sure, would have it rigged with someone, and I wondered how far he was prepared to go.

Carter pounded the desk and secured some semblance of order. He began with the little girls' baskets, most of them shoe boxes tied with red ribbon. The boys bid, bashfully and in mumbling tones: five cents, eight cents, and on up to a dime. Hardman poked me again.

"Every time I look at Wrangel I keep thinking I've seen him," Hardman said. "Wish to hell I could remember for sure, but I've got a hunch it was in Deer Lodge."

Wrangel belonged in prison all right, but I hadn't heard he'd ever been there.

Dale Oren on the other side of Hardman punched him with an elbow. He said, "Shut up. My wife's basket is coming up pretty soon and I'd better buy it or she'll never let me forget it."

Carter had reached the older girls. Four bits. Six bits. One dollar. Then the wives. The first one was a basket covered with a white linen cloth. Carter held it up and licked his lips. "Gents, I seen this one being filled this afternoon and since I know what's in it, I don't intend for nobody else to have the good eating that my missus fixed up for me." He bowed gallantly toward his wife who was sitting behind Judy. "Seeing as I'm doing all the hard work, I aim to take advantage of my position. I bid five dollars for my wife's basket, and declare the bidding closed."

Everybody clapped and Mike O'Hara whooped, "That's true love, Jesse. Is this Christmas or Valentine's Day?" Carter bowed again, set the basket to one side, and handed Susan, who was taking the money, a five-dollar gold piece. Generous, I thought, as befitted the great cowman.

Dale Oren got his wife's basket for one dollar. My father bought Susan's for a dollar and a quarter, and I wondered how she liked that. It was my guess she wanted to eat with some of the Skull crew, maybe Bud Stivers, but as the bidding went along, I noticed that nearly all the husbands got their wives' baskets with nothing more than token resistance.

The bidding stepped up when Carter reached the single

women. All except Judy were farm girls who giggled self-consciously as they eyed the cowboys. Two dollars. Two and a quarter. Russ Musil's daughter, nineteen, blond and pretty, had a huge basket that was the source of the most spirited bidding. Bud Stivers finally got it for four dollars.

"Just one left," Carter announced, "and it is a dandy. You stingy gents who have been hanging back with your hands in your pockets wrapped around your money have got just one more chance to buy your supper."

Carter held up a box that produced some exclamations of envy. It was the prettiest one that had been offered, just "so big" as Effie had measured with her hands, wrapped with white paper and tied with reams of red ribbon so that it looked like a huge rectangular stick of candy. This was Lydia Smith's, if Effie was right, but every man in the crowd thought it was Judy's because she was the only single girl left. A good many wives were here, and in the excitement, apparently no one, not even Dick Smith, had noticed that his wife's basket had not been sold.

Then suddenly the thought struck me that something had gone wrong. Where was Judy's?

15

JESSE CARTER strutted back and forth, if a man weighing three hundred pounds can be said to strut, holding the red-and-white box high for everyone to see. He hadn't received a bid, but I didn't think he expected one yet. He was a show-man, and this was the climax of the evening, so he wasn't inclined to let his big moment go too soon.

"Look at it, boys," Carter said. "Did you ever see a purtier box in all your living days than this one? By gosh, I don't believe you ever did. I'll bet that what's inside is even purtier than what's on the outside. If I hadn't bought me a box already, I wouldn't let nobody have this one. Fact is, I've got a notion . . ." He looked at his wife and shook his head. "No, I reckon one box per man is the legal limit." He got his laugh, and he called, "All right, gents, what am I bid for this beautiful box with its stummick-tickling contents?"

One of the Skull hands called, "Two dollars."

"Two dollars," Carter snorted. "Hank, I'm insulted. The last box I've got to sell and you offer me only——"

"Three dollars," I shouted, and moved forward a step.

Everybody turned and looked at me. I felt their hostility as I had so many times since the dance. Carter scowled at me as if I had done something wrong, and then, after a long moment of ominous silence, he said, "Three dollars I'm bid."

"Four," the cowboy called.

"Five," I said.

Paul Rome who was standing beside Mike O'Hara, said, "Mr. Auctioneer, we've dragged this out long enough. Everybody's hungry, so I propose to end this in order to get at the real business of the evening. I'll give you ten dollars."

Several of the boys hollered, the girls giggled, and someone in front of me said, "Why, I never heard of a basket going for ten dollars."

"That's more like it." Carter looked at me, but I made a show of pulling a pocket inside out and looking at it ruefully. "Beats me," I said, and stepped back against the wall.

"Ten dollars I'm bid by our bachelor storekeeper," Carter said. "Going once, going twice——"

"Twenty dollars," Hardman called.

Silence again, the kind of silence that was breathless. Carter swallowed. He said doubtfully, "Did I hear twenty dollars?"

"You know you did," Hardman said.

"Twenty dollars. Going once, going twice——"

"Twenty-five," Rome said.

"Thirty."

"Thirty-five."

"Forty."

"Forty-five."

"Fifty," Hardman said.

That ended it. Rome looked at O'Hara, his face white and pinched-looking around the mouth. I had no way of knowing what arrangement O'Hara had made with him, but I had an idea he'd said, "Run it up to ten dollars just to keep Bob Buel from getting it," or something of the sort. When Hardman had started the bidding, it had become personal between him and Hardman just as the hoorawing he took in his saloon every day was personal. It was my guess Rome thought this was part of the daily rawhiding that so thoroughly delighted Hardman.

Everyone knew fifty dollars was nothing to a man like Eli Hardman, but to the people in the Hole, even a storekeeper, it was a small fortune.

Rome was still looking at O'Hara. I don't know how long he stood there, probably not more than a few seconds, but it seemed as if it were a full minute. I doubt that O'Hara knew Rome was looking at him. He acted as if he'd been stunned by a blow on the head, his whiskey-befuddled brain unable to grasp what had happened. Suddenly Rome, seeing that O'Hara wasn't going to do anything, pushed through the crowd and left the building.

"Sold," Carter said weakly. "Sold to Eli Hardman for fifty dollars."

That woke O'Hara up. He let out a great bellow, and shouted, "By God, where'd I leave my jug?"

He went outside. Billy Wrangel followed, most of the other men streaming after them. In the confusion one of the little girls, the angel with the biggest wings, discovered another box everyone else had overlooked. It was in the corner behind the tree. If Carter had seen it, he probably thought it was a present for someone. At least it hadn't been placed with the rest of the baskets. The girl dragged it toward Carter, screaming, "Mr. Carter, Mr. Carter, here's another one."

Hardman was counting the money into Susan's hand. Carter, puffing like a fat pet dog that had made the mistake of taking after a jack rabbit, just stood there staring stupidly at the basket. As I started up the aisle, I saw that this one was almost identical to the basket Hardman had bought, but the difference was significant. A doll was tied into the bow of ribbon, a little doll with a blue bonnet and a red dress.

The angel girl kept tugging at Carter's coat tail. "Here's another one, Mr. Carter." He looked at her as if he hated both her and the basket. He had neither the will nor the energy to go through this again, I thought, and when I said, "I'll give you three dollars," he looked at me as if he had never seen me before. He said mechanically, "Sold."

By the time I picked up the basket, Hardman had finished paying Susan. I handed her three silver dollars, and I could not mistake the malice that was in her voice when she said, "You got the wrong basket, Bob. Isn't that too bad?"

I said nothing. My father, standing beside Susan, was silent, too, his eyes on the floor as if studying something there. I turned away, fumbling with the ribbon. Before I got the lid off, Hardman had found Mrs. Smith's name inside his basket and was bowing to her, saying, "I expect you to eat this good grub with me, Mrs. Smith."

"Of course I will. I'm hungry." She stood up and looked around. "I fixed enough for my husband, too, but he isn't here. I'll bet he's outside getting drunk with Mike O'Hara."

By that time I had found Judy's name inside the basket, and when I went to her, she said, "Why, Mr. Buel, this is a surprise, you buying my basket."

"I'll bet it is," I said, and could not keep from glancing at Susan who was standing staring at me, her mouth open.

Hardman said, "Ma'am, if your husband ain't handy, and if you fixed plenty, maybe it would be all right for my partner to eat with us. Sam Logan. You know him, I reckon."

"Of course," she said resignedly, and I had a feeling she had already regretted her part in the trickery.

The children were diving into their shoe boxes and filling their mouths as if they hadn't eaten all day, but for everybody else in the room, the actual eating was anticlimax. It didn't bother Hardman or Logan; and I pretended to enjoy Judy's food. She had fried chicken just as Mrs. Smith had promised. There were sandwiches and two jars of salmon salad and huge servings of the three-layer cake with whipped cream that was Dick Smith's favorite, according to his wife.

When I told Judy dutifully that everything was wallopin' good larrupin', she said, "Don't give me any credit, Bob. Lydia fixed everything."

Mrs. Smith was distressed, her eyes moving constantly to the door. She said, "Don't believe a word of it, Mr. Buel. She helped. Besides, she worked all day on my dress. Worked like a dog."

If Judy shared Lydia Smith's alarm, she gave no hint whatever. I had never seen anyone's eyes sparkle the way her blue ones did. She was enjoying the whole business, particularly her father's and Paul Rome's discomfiture, I thought, but when I said, "I'd like to ride home with you," she bit her lower lip, her face turning grave. She glanced at the door, then brought her gaze to my face as she laid a hand on my arm.

"I wish you could, Bob, but it wouldn't do, especially after what happened tonight. I do want to see you again, though. I've got to talk to you, but we'd better wait. I'll let you know."

I nodded, understanding her reason for putting me off. I got up and looked down at her, and again I thought how beautiful she was and how important it was that I see her again. I said, "Don't let anything stop you. Not anything."

She smiled, letting me know that our seeing each other was just as important to her as it was to me. "I won't," she said.

Hardman delicately wiped the last bit of whipped cream off his mustache when I asked, "Ready to go?"

"Sure he's ready," Logan said. "He ate everything in sight."

Mrs. Smith's hands were fluttering on her lap, her eyes still straying to the door. She said, "I hope you men had plenty to eat. My goodness, I never dreamed that my basket would sell for . . . for fifty dollars."

"It was worth twice that, ma'am," Hardman said, and bowed to her.

We started down the aisle toward the door, but we hadn't gone ten feet when Carter called, "Hardman."

We stopped as Carter heaved his great bulk off the bench where he'd been sitting with his wife. He came to us, wiping his coat sleeve across his greasy mouth. Hardman said, "If you're still hungry, Jesse, I can't help you. I had to divvy up my supper with this long-legged polecat with the appetite." He motioned toward Logan. "Left me short. Fact is, if you've got an extra drumstick . . ."

"I don't." Carter had been working himself up to this, and Hardman's levity put him off balance. He wiped his mouth again. "I ain't joshing and you'd better listen. We've put up with your kind in the Hole 'cause some folks make money and they wouldn't like it if we ran you out. That's the only reason we let you stay. If you had any sense, you'd know that, but tonight you went sticking your nose into a place where it didn't belong. You do it again and we'll run you right over the pass, snow or no snow." He looked at me. "And you, too, Buel."

Logan began to swear. Hardman rammed an elbow into his stomach. "Shut up, Sam." Hardman nodded at Carter. "You do that, Jesse. You just do that."

Hardman went on toward the door. Logan jumped ahead of him so that he reached the door first. As he opened it, his hand still on the knob, he said, "You letting old Lard Keg talk that kind of medicine?"

"Sure I am," Hardman said. "He's right. We shouldn't have let Effie talk us into this."

Hardman went through the door and I followed. For an instant I was framed there with the light behind me. In that exact moment a gun cut loose from across the road. Even as I dived headlong into the yard away from the door, the thought ran through my mind that it was Wrangel who had shot at me, and only a miracle would keep one of the women or children behind me from getting hit.

I heard the door slam shut. Logan had that much presence of mind. Inside the schoolhouse someone was screaming, but it was a scream of fear, not of pain. My gun was in my hand, my body flat on the frozen ground. Hardman, somewhere off to my right, called, "You all right, Bob?"

I didn't answer. I got up and ran forward, my boots clattering on the hard ground. Wrangel was on his feet running toward me, shooting wildly, perhaps because he sensed that when he had missed his one good shot, he had declared himself a dead man. When I caught the vague, shadowy bulk of his big body, I fired three times, fast, and threw myself sideways. I lay there, holding back the remaining two bullets in my gun.

Silence then that seemed to ribbon on and on endlessly. Presently the men who had been drinking outside the schoolhouse began drifting forward, and I heard O'Hara's voice, "What happened?" And Hardman, "You son of a bitch, you ought to know. You put Wrangel out here to plug Buel when he came through the door."

"I didn't do nothing of the kind," O'Hara said indignantly. "It wasn't Billy. Must have been somebody else."

"Let's go see," Hardman said. "I think Buel got him. I didn't hear him running away, but maybe he crawled off."

Logan came out of the schoolhouse, closing the door. When he came toward me, I stood up. "Anybody hurt?"

"No," he said savagely, "but I don't know why."

We moved across the road, slowly, O'Hara calling, "If that's you, Billy, don't move. It's me."

Wrangel wasn't moving anywhere unless someone else did the moving. He lay on his stomach, his face cheek down on a sheet of ice. One of my bullets had caught him in the chest, another had sliced through his belly. The third had missed completely.

We stood there a moment: O'Hara, Dick Smith, Dale Oren, Bud Stivers, and several others. Finally I said, "O'Hara, I told you that if he tried again, I'd kill him."

"Damned lucky shooting," Stivers muttered.

"That's right," I said. "Plain luck, but he's dead just the same, and I killed him. What about it, O'Hara?"

"What can he say?" Hardman asked. "You put Wrangel up to it, didn't you, O'Hara?"

He had been shocked cold-sober, for he had held a match close to the dead man's face. He said dully, "I didn't know anything about it, but I ain't gonna forget you done it, Buel, if that's what you're wanting to know. It was a bad day for all of us when you rode over the pass. Dale, go get your team. We'll take him home. And Dick, have your wife take Judy home with her."

He sounded like a sick man. For the first time I had some notion of the strange bond of affection that had existed between him and the dead man. I started toward the hotel, Hardman and Logan falling into step with me. Then, quite suddenly, it struck me that Hardman's and Logan's presence might have saved me from trouble again.

At least they had sided me, and they had incurred Jesse Carter's displeasure by buying the basket. So I owed them a little more than I had before. Bounty chaser, I thought bitterly, a Judas man.

As soon as we reached the hotel, I went upstairs to bed, but I could not sleep. For the first time I gave serious thought to forgetting all about my bargain with Jason Harwig. I owed him nothing. I had not taken a lawman's oath. I could get along without the thousand dollars. When the pass was open, I would simply ride out of Dirken's Hole and keep on going. There would be other jobs to do, other men to bring in. As far as Hardman and Logan were concerned, Harwig could do his own dirty work.

16

By THE last of January I had caught up with all the work I could find to do around the hotel. I was even ahead on the wood, with a month's supply piled up in the shed. In spite of myself, I found it hard to be civil to Hardman and Logan, realizing I was more beholden to them than ever. I didn't want to drink with them in Rome's place. Or play poker. Or even sit and talk.

Effie was plainly impatient with me. She had some clabbered milk and was making smearcase one cold Sunday afternoon when I wandered into the kitchen. There wasn't even a book to read in the hotel, and I wasn't of a mind to ask Paul Rome for one. Going to my father was out of the question.

"Sit down, Bob," Effie said. "You've been acting like you've got ants in your pants and they've multiplied since the Christmas party."

I sat down at the table and rolled a smoke. I was willing to let her think I was jumpy because I hadn't heard from Judy. That actually was part of the trouble. More than four weeks had passed since Judy had said she had to talk to me, that she'd let me know. So far I had heard nothing, not even in a roundabout way from Lydia Smith. That hurt.

In all honesty I had to admit there were factors I could not evaluate. I knew Billy Wrangel had been buried on the O'Hara ranch, and that Dale Oren had been hired to work for O'Hara. That was all I did know because neither O'Hara nor Judy had come to the settlement, so I had no way of knowing how O'Hara felt toward me, now that some time had passed since the shooting, or what he would do if I rode out there to see Judy. I tried to tell myself she knew what she was doing, that she couldn't defy her father just now. But there were other days when I felt I was fooling myself, that I didn't really know whether Judy gave two whoops and a holler about me or not.

Effie looked at me from the pantry door. "If you're eating your heart out on account of Judy, why in hell don't you ride out there and get it over with?"

"If I rode out there now," I said, "I might get it over with, sudden like and permanent, so I figure I'll wait."

I couldn't tell her, of course, that I was so mixed up inside that sometimes my food lay like a rock in my stomach. I couldn't tell her I had come to the Hole to make a thousand dollars and as soon as the pass was open, I had to take Hardman and Logan prisoners and march them out to a louse-infested jail and turn them over to some sadistic jailer who'd give them slop for food, then they'd come up for trial and get twenty years in the pen. No, I couldn't tell that to anyone, but I would have felt better if I could.

Effie came out of the pantry and sat down at the table. She probably thought I was lovesick like a teen-age kid. She tapped the table with her big, bony fingers, then she stuck out her lower lip at me. "Bob, you holding against me what happened at the Christmas party? I didn't know that Wrangel would try to plug you."

I knew then it had been bothering her all this time, and I said quickly, "No, I haven't been holding it against you. It had to come sooner or later. I just feel lucky he didn't get me."

She took a long breath and fidgeted around as though she was laboring with her thoughts, and finally she said, "I never held with this business of marrying because you were in love. Men get married because they want a woman in bed with 'em and to cook for 'em and such, and women get married so they'll have a man to earn a living and make 'em important in the community like Susan hankered for."

This was typical of Effie's cynical attitude toward love and marriage, and I knew she had reason to feel that way. She'd said enough about her marriage for me to know it had been an unhappy one. Living in the same house with Link and Susan had strengthened her opinion. There were times when I felt the same way, but then I would remember how it had been with my father and mother and I knew there was such a thing as love, and the man and woman who had it were lucky indeed.

I sat there, not arguing with her and not agreeing, either. Then she said, "But I figure it's different with you and Judy. You've just got to ride out there and lay your cards on the table."

"What cards?"

"Bob Buel, you make me so damned mad sometimes. Maybe you don't know it, but you're in love with her. Go out there and tell her. Tell Mike, too. There's times if you catch him right he ain't unreasonable."

"Effie, you're talking through your hat. You don't believe there's such a thing as love."

That made her furious. I don't know what she would have said if Hardman and Logan hadn't stomped in, Hardman waving a tattered piece of paper in his hand. Both of them looked too smug to suit me, and it was only a moment before I found out what was working on them.

"Listen to this, Effie," Hardman crowed. "I got something to read to you." He held up the piece of paper. "Bob Buel, alias the Ochoco Kid, alias Ben Ball. Wanted for train robbery. One thousand dollars reward."

I lunged out of my chair, and grabbing the paper out of his hand, wadded it up and threw it into the stove. "Where'd you get it?" I demanded.

Of course Hardman and Logan thought it was funny. Logan said, "The teacher's law-abiding son! What would Tom Buel say if he seen that?"

"You tell him and I'll make you wish you'd never seen it yourself," I said. "You savvy?"

They stopped laughing when they discovered I was taking this more seriously than they expected. Effie said, "Cool down, Bob. I'm to blame. I found it when I was putting your clothes away. I was gonna ask you about it, so I put it on top of your bureau, figuring you'd be sure to see it. Then, damn it, I plumb forgot. I ain't surprised, you understand. Everybody in the Hole figures you had some reason for wintering here besides just seeing your dad."

I sat down, hit hard by what she had just said. "Everybody?" I asked.

Hardman and Logan pulled chairs back from the table and sat down. Hardman said, "Maybe we should of told you. You'd be the last to know. We heard it just after you got to the Hole. Rome told us and he got it from Susan. Seems like she found one of them dodgers in your clothes while you were staying there."

I should have known. I did, really, I think. She must have

shown it to my father. That had been the reason he'd turned against me. He probably thought, just as Effie had said, that everybody knew, and that I'd ruined his reputation.

"You got no cause to get down in the mouth," Effie said. "It's got nothing to do with Judy, if she likes you. Fact is, Mike's been the one more'n anybody who says let 'em stay here long as they don't bother nobody."

Logan winked at me. "Mike'll swap horses with you every time if it'll make him ten dollars. Same as Effie, and he'll skin you to death like she will, too, if he gets a chance."

"Don't get snibberty," Effie snapped. "I didn't ask you two to live here."

"Paul Rome don't ask us to drink his whiskey, neither," Hardman said. "Real good folks here in the Hole, Bob, long as they can make something off of us."

"It ain't as bad as you're letting on," Effie said indignantly. "We like to be let alone, that's all. We don't want no big out-side spreads pushing their cows down here or sending their back-shooting exterminators in here to murder us like Har-wig done Link. We don't need their God-damned law to get along with each other."

This was exactly what Jason Harwig had meant when he'd called Dirken's Hole "half-outlaw" country. I would be far better off to be considered a ridge runner like Hardman and Logan than to have the truth come out. Still, I wished I had destroyed the reward dodgers. They had given Susan a weapon she had been only too happy to use against me. By telling Rome, she had started the story which undoubtedly had spread all over the Hole.

Hardman and Logan were uneasy, now that they had had their fun. They were silent, watching me covertly. Finally Hardman said, "I looked into your room to see if you was there. Thought we might get a little poker going, then I seen this paper and I picked it up." He laughed shortly. "From the back side it looked kind o' familiar."

"Not from the other side, though," Logan said. "Had a good-looking face on it instead of your ugly mug."

"Yeah, real handsome," Hardman said.

In their way they were asking to be forgiven. I suppose they hadn't thought how I'd take it. Maybe I wouldn't have been sore if I hadn't been jumpy anyway. I said, "Forget it. I was loco for packing those things around with me."

"Oh, I dunno," Hardman said. "We all do. I've got five, six of 'em rolled up in my gear. Tear 'em off every telegraph pole I see 'em on. Kind of gives a man satisfaction to know he's worth a thousand dollars to somebody."

"A purty piddling price," Logan mused. "We got fifty thousand in our saddle bags upstairs, but to the railroad we're only worth one thousand."

"That's your railroad for you," Hardman said. "A real tinhorn outfit. I'll tell you, Bob. Why don't you ride out with us, come spring? Me'n Sam kind o' like the cut of your jib."

Hardman's pale blue eyes were on me, and for a moment I thought he was trying to trap me, that he knew the truth and was giving me all the rope I needed. I had no illusions about either Hardman or Logan. So far they had been very pleasant, but under the right circumstances, they would be the most ruthless men I had ever faced.

I finally decided I was imagining things, so I said, "Thanks, Eli, but I'm quitting."

"Quitting, he says." Hardman winked at Logan. "You ever hear of a man quitting?"

"Not to stay quit," Logan answered.

"That's it in a nutshell," Hardman agreed. "I've quit ten times, but I always go back. Why, a man's a fool to work when there's banks and trains to rob. Don't hurt my conscience none, neither. They're robbers, if you want to look at it fair'n square. Nobody ever got big without making the little man smaller. Railroads. Banks. Big cattle outfits. All the same. They get their start by stealing, then after they once get their wad, they don't have to steal no more. They're respectable."

"You gonna take that fifty thousand and be respectable?" Effie laughed.

Hardman grinned. "No sir. After living like we have this winter, we're heading for Denver to buy ourselves a time. When we're broke, we'll start looking for another train."

"Or a bank," Logan said. "I kind o' cotton to banks. It's all piled up just waiting for us to come along and take it."

"You'll never beat it," Effie said. "You could live here the rest of your lives and be safe. Or sneak down into Mexico and buy a hacienda, but you ain't that smart. You'll wind up on the end of a rope or with lead poisoning."

"Short and sweet," Logan said. "That's the way we live. What about it, Bob?"

"No, I'm quitting," I said. "There's something in what Effie says. Maybe it's time I was settling down."

"And turning respectable," Hardman said disgustedly. "Well, every dog to his own poison, but what some dogs will eat sure turns a man's stummick."

His pale eyes were on me again, and I wondered how long I could fool a man like him, or if I was fooling him at all. I was relieved when Effie said, "Quit pestering him. He don't know it, but he's in love with Judy O'Hara. A man can't get married and ride the owlhoot."

Logan slapped me on the back. "Sure, I seen it coming the time we took Wrangel over there and Judy was looking down that scattergun barrel. She was in love with him right then, but Bob here wasn't real sure. Hard to tell, looking at a purty girl with buckshot standing between you."

Hardman got up. "You're getting mushy, Sam. Let's go see Rome. Maybe that quick heat of his will warm us up."

After they left, Effie said, "They're all alike, easy come, easy go. But you're different, Bob. Don't let 'em talk you into it again. You'll get things fixed up with Judy. You'll see."

"I aim to," I said, and got up and left the house.

I went out to the wood pile and started chopping for lack of anything else to do. Suddenly I was glad it had happened this way. I could quit worrying about taking Hardman and Logan in. No matter what they had done for me personally, they hadn't changed and they never would. I didn't know how many men they had killed in the past, but if they kept on robbing trains or banks, they'd kill more men who had families that loved them. If a bank went broke because it was robbed, dozens of innocent men would go down with the banker. It would never stop as long as they were free.

So I could quit thinking about my personal debt to Hardman and Logan. At least I told myself I could. I had never yet failed to do a job that had been given me; and I wouldn't fail this one when the time came.

Hardman and Logan could justify themselves all they

wanted to, but their arguments made no impression on me. Law was law, a crime was a crime, and the doer of a crime must be punished. Yet I would not forget that I owed the greatest debt a man could owe to Eli Hardman and Sam Logan. The fact that they were train robbers and I was a professional man-hunter did not change that situation. So the doubt lingered.

17

THE FIRST week in February brought a heavy snow, the worst Effie had ever seen in the Hole. For two days the wind howled around the hotel with a savage, spine-twisting screech. The snow fell steadily for forty-eight hours, but it was impossible to tell how much we had on the level because the wind wouldn't let it alone. So, on the third day when the sun came out to shine with blinding brilliance, we had a strange, lumpy world, with the ground bare in spots, and snowdrifts ten feet high in other places.

All transportation came to a standstill for a week. My father didn't even attempt to hold school. I met him in the store at the end of that week, the first time I had seen him since the Christmas party.

He was just leaving as I went in, the fur flaps of his cap over his ears, his coat collar pulled up around his neck. He said, "Good morning, Robert," and would have gone on if I hadn't reached out and barred his progress with my arm. I had not forgotten that he'd told me to stay out of his way, but there was a look about him that alarmed me, a gray pallor that would only be on the face of a sick man.

"How are you feeling?" I asked.

He squared his shoulders in an effort to be defiant. He said, "I feel fine."

For a moment our eyes met, then he lowered his gaze, and I wondered if he felt as miserable as I did. I was thinking of the day after my mother had died, and my father and I had nooned at the junction of Dirken's and July Creeks. He'd said, "I have a feeling my destiny is here. . . . Regardless of how much I need you, I can't ask you to stay."

Perhaps he was glad I hadn't. He was plainly sorry I had come back. I suppose a father and son never understood each other, for by nature we must be of two generations, one with most of his life behind him, the other just beginning his. But our trouble was more than lack of understanding. I had every right to hate him, it seemed to me, but I didn't. My feeling was one of pity, and I asked, "Is there anything I can do for you?"

He did not look at me. He said, "Nothing," and I dropped my arm and let him go. Russ Musil was in the store, and I listened to his talk for a time, neither Musil nor Rome acting as if they knew I existed.

"No doubt about it, Paul," Musil said. "This is the toughest winter since I've been in the Hole, and that's been sixteen year, come next June."

"Worst I can remember," Rome agreed.

"Must be thirty feet of snow on the pass," Musil said. "It'll be closed till July."

They were just talking, Musil backed up against the red-hot stove, Rome standing behind the counter. Anger took hold of me. I stepped between them. "Rome," I said, "Effie wants five pounds of dried peaches, some crackers, and a pound of coffee."

Rome stood there, not moving. Musil said, "You've got mighty bad manners, Buel. It's gonna get you in trouble one of these days."

"You'll wait on me, Rome," I said, "or I'll be on the other side of the counter and you'll wish you had."

Rome's little mouth began to work the way it did when he was angry at Hardman and Logan, but he turned and started weighing out the peaches. I remained squarely in front of Musil, my back to him. If he'd made another remark, I'd have turned around and knocked him down. I think he knew it. At least he didn't open his mouth as long as I was in the store. Rome finished filling my order and made out the charge slip.

I watched him and when he was done, I said, "Your prices are going up, Rome."

He looked at me, only he didn't actually pin his eyes on me. He said, "It's the law of supply and demand."

I said, "If you don't get a rope on your neck about April, I'll be surprised."

I walked out, my temper boiling. I found Effie in the

89

kitchen and gave her the things she'd ordered. "Unless you want something done," I said, "I'm taking a ride."

"Go right ahead," she said. "Be good for you to get out. You look mad at something."

"I am," I said. "Look at Rome's prices."

"I don't need to. I can pay, but what's gonna happen to Smith and Oren and Musil and the rest of 'em?"

"They'll starve," I said, and went out to the barn and saddled my buckskin.

I didn't really intend to go to the O'Hara ranch when I started, but I headed in that direction, then I thought about it and decided Effie was right, that I had to go out there and lay my cards on the table. I'd been hoping to get word from Judy, but I hadn't. O'Hara's fault I was sure.

Still, if Judy felt about me the way I felt about her, she'd find a way to see me. And how did I feel about her? Effie said I was in love. I didn't know. I had no way of knowing. I'd never given much thought to getting married, but Judy seemed to be the kind of woman I wanted. I kept riding.

I made a late start, and I had to ride around snowdrifts time after time, so it was mid-afternoon when I reached the O'Hara place. I tied in front of the house, noting that a pillar of smoke rose from the chimney into the cold, motionless air. Judy would be there, I thought, but I should see O'Hara first. If I had trouble with him, I'd rather have it when Judy wasn't around.

This was the kind of day when sound carried on and on. Someone was in the barn talking. O'Hara and Oren probably, I thought. I crossed the yard, opened the barn door, and went in. O'Hara and Oren had brought in some sick ewes and were standing talking about them, their backs to me.

"Howdy," I said, and they spun around. Oren looked frightened when he saw me, and O'Hara's red-veined face turned redder than ever.

"Well?" O'Hara said.

I walked across the straw-littered floor of the barn, glad that I wasn't wearing my gun. O'Hara could not mistake my errand for one of violence. He stood with his stubby legs spread, hostility written all over him.

I said, "I want your permission to call on Judy."

"I wouldn't give you permission to step on my property," he said harshly.

"Then I'll see her without your permission," I said. "She's a grown woman, O'Hara, and that gives her a right to make up her own mind. If she says she doesn't want to see me, I'll never bother her again."

"You won't see her." He took a step toward me, then stopped. I wasn't sure whether he remembered what had happened to Billy Wrangel and was afraid, or whether he thought of Judy. He pulled at his beard, looking squarely at me, then he said, "Buel, I've lived here better'n twenty years. Judy was born on this ranch. My wife died on the same bed she gave birth to Judy on and she's buried yonder where Billy is.

"Ridge runners like you and Hardman and Logan have gone through here by the dozen. They've never bothered us and we didn't bother them. We've never had what folks call law in the Hole, and we don't need it." He swallowed, and jabbed a thick forefinger in my direction. "But since you got here we've had nothing but trouble. Can you tell me how one man could stir up a hornets' nest like you have, and why he'd do it?"

I hesitated. "No, I can't tell you," I said finally, "but none of it was of my choosing. Now maybe you can tell me something. When I first met you the night of the dance, you were friendly. Then you decided I was poison. Why?"

He bowed his great head and scratched a toe through the litter on the ground. Oren said, "Tell him, Mike."

I was surprised at that, but when I looked at Oren, his face told me nothing. Then O'Hara raised his head. "All right, I'll tell you. Tom Buel is a good man, the best school teacher we ever had in the Hole. I figured his son would be as good, but when I heard you was just another outlaw on the dodge, taking advantage of your dad to winter here, I didn't want you smelling around Judy."

"You heard it from Susan?"

"From Paul Rome. He got it from Susie."

I could not tell them she had lied, not after Hardman and Logan had found the reward dodger. O'Hara wouldn't believe me, anyway. He was, as Effie had often stated it, a stiff-necked and proudful man.

91

"Suppose you trust me till summer," I said. "Is that too much to ask?"

"Trust you?" He threw back his head and brayed a laugh at me. "I wouldn't trust you to carry a shovelful of sheep manure across the barn. When I found out what you was, I wanted Billy to stomp your guts out. And I ain't forgot it was you that got the drop on him and fetched him here with Hardman and Logan backing you up. Just to look big in front of Judy, I reckon. She cottoned to you right off. I saw that. Don't ask me why. A woman can make an awful fool of herself over a man. I don't aim for Judy to do it over you. Now get out of here and don't stop at the house."

"You know Wrangel tried to kill me the night of the Christmas party."

"You pushed him into it," O'Hara said harshly, "and then you killed him. He was a good herder and he was my friend."

He was visibly shaken by his fury. If I stayed, there would be a fight that would gain nothing for either of us, so I whirled and walked out, closing the door behind me. For a moment I stood staring at the house, wanting to see Judy more than I had ever wanted to see anyone in my life. But I couldn't. Not today. I would manage it later, somehow. So I walked across the frozen yard that had been swept clear of snow by the wind and mounted and rode away.

I did not look back. I was afraid I'd see Judy at a window. If I had, I would have returned to talk to her, then I would have trouble with O'Hara, the kind of trouble that might separate me from Judy forever. I rode with my head down, the reins held loosely in my hand, my mind fixed so intently upon my problem that I was not aware I had crossed a greasewood flat and had started up a dry wash. I was entirely unprepared for Judy's voice, "How are you, Bob?"

I must have looked ridiculous, almost jumping out of my saddle and yanking my buckskin to a stop. She was sitting her saddle astride a bay pony, both gloved hands folded over the horn, a wool cap pulled down over her ears. She was laughing silently, pleased, I think, at the start she had given me.

"I thought you were in the house?" I said.

"You mean you didn't stop to see?"

"I talked to your dad," I said. "I asked permission to see

you and he said he wouldn't give me permission to step on his property. I figured that if I stopped, we'd have more trouble. I knew I'd have heard from you before now if it wasn't for him. That's right, isn't it?"

She didn't answer for a moment. Her face turned grave, her eyes searching my face for some assurance of my feeling, I think, then she said slowly, "That's right. It's been hard living here since that night. He wanted to take a gun and go after you, and I told him I'd leave and never come back." The tip of her pink tongue touched her lips. She asked, "Bob, when you're grown and you know your own mind and what you want from life, how much do you still owe your father?"

"I'm twenty-five," I said, "and I still don't know the answer to that question."

"I know, I know. It was silly of me to ask." She looked down the slope toward the buildings, biting her lower lip, and I waited, for I sensed that she was working toward a decision, one she must reach herself. Then she looked at me, smiling again. "I had nothing to do with Lydia's and Effie's scheming to get us together at the Christmas party."

"I knew you didn't," I said.

"It worked out badly as they should have known it would," she went on. "Hardman and Logan shouldn't have come to the party and bought Lydia's basket. It made Dick mad and he's been taking it out on her ever since. And it was bad because it made Billy try to kill you and you had to kill him. Mike can't get over that."

"There seem to be a lot of unwritten laws around here," I said. "For men like Hardman and Logan."

She knew, of course, that I was placed in the same category by the people of the Hole. She nodded, and I sensed that it was in her mind but she didn't want to actually put it into words. She said, "I'm to blame for you coming to the party. I should have known better, too, but—well, I guess I didn't think very clearly about it."

She was hedging because she couldn't come right out and say she wanted me to buy her basket. I said quickly, "It isn't right for us not to see each other because your dad's bullheaded."

"No," she said softly, "it isn't, and I'm wicked enough

to fool him. I have a right to. I can't go on living like I have been, in prison this way. That's what it amounts to. Sometimes I think I'll go crazy and start screaming."

I looked at the high east wall, bare of snow except where it had caught in cracks or patches of brush that clung precariously to the shallow soil. I said, "I think I'll go crazy, just spending one winter here."

"Bob," she said with finality as if she had at last reached the decision toward which she had been groping, "there's a rock cabin three miles south of here that's vacant, but it's tight and comfortable enough. It's right up against the cliff. Could you find it?"

"Sure I could."

"I'll be there a week from Sunday, if the weather's good."

"I'll be there, too," I said.

She smiled again and nodded and rode away. I went on toward the settlement, feeling a serenity I had not felt for weeks.

18

THE LAST half of February turned off warm and the snow disappeared except on the foothills and high mountains to the south. A feeling of spring was in the air, and it seemed to me that the buds on the big cottonwoods in front of the hotel were beginning to swell.

"Time to get your garden in, Effie," I said. "Want me to plow it for you?"

"Hell no," Effie said. "Might be snowing by Sunday. Put seed in the ground now and it'll rot."

Surely it wouldn't snow by Sunday, I thought. That was the day I would meet Judy in the rock cabin at the foot of the rim. Then I wondered if the weather as well as Mike O'Hara was against me.

Despite the warm days, the nights remained cold so that we needed a fire in the evenings. On the Friday night before the Sunday I was to meet Judy I was sprawled on the battered leather couch in the front room of the hotel when Hardman and Logan came downstairs.

"Want to play a little poker?" Hardman asked.

"Can't afford it," I said. "I don't have fifty thousand to lose like you boys do."

That was a standing joke. They'd spend hours playing cards in their rooms, betting thousands of dollars on a single hand. On two occasions at least Hardman had the entire fifty thousand, but that didn't stop them. They simply divided the money equally between them and started over.

Hardman laughed as he pulled a rocking chair up to the Franklin stove and sat down, his legs stretched toward the fire. "You could have it, too, if you wanted to throw in with us."

Logan sat down on the floor beside the stove and lighted a cigar. "Eli, remember the time we was holed up in Robber's Roost? Had better'n fifty thousand, but it was all in greenbacks and there was four of us. Before we got out, we gambled with them greenbacks so much we had the pictures plumb wore off."

Hardman laughed again. "Yeah, and I remember the posse that came in after us and we took their pants off 'em. They had to walk twenty miles across the desert into town in their drawers."

Logan snickered. "That sheriff didn't even run again. Folks just naturally laughed him right off the ticket."

Hardman was studying the stove. "Ever notice them faces, Bob?" He pointed a stubby finger at the right side of the stove where a half-moon face grimaced as if it had tasted something sour. "The gent that rigged them up was a smart man. That one is all the mean no-good sons of bitches that are in the world. The railroad owners and bankers and big cowmen who hire exterminators like Jason Harwig. That's the marshals and the sheriffs and the bounty chasers. There's nothing lower'n a bounty chaser."

He glanced covertly at me to see how I was taking his lecture, and again I had the feeling he wasn't fooled at all, that he knew what I was and had been playing a cat-and-mouse game with me right from the first. But I had reached a point where I refused to worry. I still had at least three months before the pass would be open.

Logan was studying the faces. "You know, Eli, that is a mean-looking cuss, but the other one's happy."

"He's all the good people in the world," Hardman said.

"He's the hard-working, ordinary poor devil who has to buck the rich boogers. He's the train robbers and bank robbers like us, Sam, who take money from them that has it and gives it to them who don't."

Effie had finished the supper dishes and had come into the room in time to hear the last chapter of Hardman's dissertation. She snorted her derision. "You mean the floozies and gamblers and saloon keepers, don't you?"

"I'd include them," Hardman agreed, his cynical little smile barely visible behind his mustache. "Take the girls you call floozies. Can you think of anyone who gives a man more pleasure than they do?"

"That's right," Logan said enthusiastically. "Why don't you keep a few floozies on hand, Effie?"

Effie put her hands on her hips and scorched Logan with a look. "Mister, when I get that low down, you can just mark me off. I'm done."

I don't think Hardman heard. He was staring at the evil face on the stove. "That hombre looks just like Paul Rome. I was in the saloon today when Dick Smith came in and asked for credit. You think he got it, even at the prices Rome's charging? No he didn't. If them farmers weren't a bunch of old women, they'd take that store apart."

"There's your floozy for you," Effie said triumphantly. "Susie's putting him up to it. Wouldn't surprise me none if they pull out together next summer with Rome taking everything he's able to steal this winter."

I sat up. "What are you talking about?"

"I'm talking about Susan Castle Buel," Effie said. "She's been living with Paul Rome off and on ever since she's been here. I knew it when Link was alive, but he was like your dad, too trusting to believe anything wrong about his wife."

I looked at Effie, not wanting to believe this, but I had never known her to lie. Still, Paul Rome with his pale face and soft hands and little pot belly didn't seem the kind of man who would appeal to a woman like Susan. I said so and Effie just threw up her hands.

"Don't expect me to explain a thing like that. Maybe he's more stud horse than he looks. When Link was alive I was sure scared he'd find out. Not that I cared about Paul Rome living a long life. I just didn't want Link to get into trouble.

We hadn't had a killing here for years. It might have brung the sheriff in and we sure didn't want that." She laughed shortly. "Well, me and Susie had quite a fight over it. We went all around the kitchen, pulling hair and biting and gouging. I whopped her all right, but I didn't change her. Nothing's ever gonna change that devil."

"You always said Rome used every nickel he had to trap another one," I argued. "I don't see why you're blaming his cussedness on Susan."

"You holding up for her?" Effie challenged.

"No, but you've said time and time again that she wanted to be respectable. Sneaking off to sleep with Paul Rome wouldn't make her respectable."

Effie scratched her fat nose as if that thought hadn't occurred to her. "Don't jibe for a fact," she admitted, "but I reckon Susie thinks she can fool everybody. Anyhow, she's the kind who wants something till she gets it and then she doesn't want it. You're trying to make it logical, but there just ain't nothing logical about Susie."

Hardman and Logan had been listening. Now they got up, Hardman asking, "Bob, did you ever smoke a bear out of his cave?"

"Never did," I answered.

"Well, sir, it's more fun than taking pants off a sheriff," Hardman said, "but it's trickier. You find their cave, see? You wait till the she-bear and the he-bear lie down together, then after they've got their fire going, you climb up on top of the cave and plug up their chimney. That's when the real fun commences."

"Sounds like snipe hunting," I said.

"Aw, it's more dangerous than snipe hunting," Hardman said. "Take the she-bear now. She'll come out of the cave a-ripping and a-snorting. You get in her way and she'll claw your eyes out every time."

Logan asked innocently, "Any bears around here we can smoke out?"

Hardman stroked one side of his mustache, then the other as he thoughtfully considered the question. Finally he said, "Yeah, I know a couple."

"Well, let's get at it," Logan said.

"It's dangerous," Hardman said hesitantly. "How about you, Bob?"

I shook my head. "It's warm here and cold outside."

Logan walked to the rack beside the door and put his coat on. "Aw, come on, Bob. We'll do all the work."

"I can hold the bag for the snipe," I said.

"That's about it," Hardman agreed blandly, "only I said this was dangerous."

"You didn't believe me," Effie said belligerently. "Now go find out for yourself."

Under the circumstances with Effie glaring at me, her hands on her hips, I couldn't very well refuse. I got up, put on my coat and Hardman grabbed his and we went through the front door. The moon was a sliver, but the sky was clear and the stars were out, so we had some light.

Hardman said, "Sam, you get them boards behind the barn. I'll fetch the ladder. Bob, you just stand at the back door of the store."

"How do you know the she-bear's there?" I asked.

"Guessing," Hardman admitted. "This is Friday night. Rome's supposed to close up at eight except on Saturdays, but most nights he'll let us stay as long as we want to. Come Friday it's different. He runs us out at eight right on the dot."

I left them, circling the store and going around to the back-door that opened into Rome's living quarters. I had never been inside, but Effie had told me how it was. Rome's father had built the place when there were only three or four settlers in the Hole.

"He was an honest man," Effie told me, "and he worked hard. He lost his wife and he spoiled Paul, but I reckon he done his best. Built on the lean-to so he'd have a saloon. Fetched in some nice furniture. There's a bedroom and kitchen and a real fancy parlor. But Paul's a purty thin sliver off a solid old block."

I was thinking of this as I stood shivering by the back door. Now I doubted my good sense in having any part of the deal. Hardman and Logan might be taking me for a snipe hunt. It would fit their notion of humor.

I don't know how long I waited. I wouldn't have stayed as long as I did if it hadn't been for Effie. She wouldn't lie, even prejudiced as she was against Susan, but she might be

98

mistaken. I had almost no respect for Susan and yet this thing of sneaking out of my father's house to come to Paul Rome was too much for me to believe. I had to know, so I waited.

When I left the hotel, it had not occurred to me to see what time it was and now I could not risk lighting a match to look at my watch. I decided it must be after midnight and I might just as well go back, when I heard someone moving around inside, then a spell of coughing, and I heard Susan cry, "Do something, Paul. The place must be on fire. I can't breathe."

So it was true. I didn't leave because I wondered what Rome would do. It would take him all night to figure out that someone had placed boards over the chimney. I heard more coughing, then a lamp was lighted, and Susan said, "I'm not going to stay and burn to death. Do something!"

"Must be the damper," Rome said. "Open the back door and let some of this smoke out."

The back door opened. When I saw that Susan had nothing on but her nightgown, I was suddenly so angry I acted on impulse. I grabbed her by an arm and yanked her through the door and onto the cold, trodden earth behind the store. She screamed. I don't know whether there was enough light for her to recognize me or not, but she was scared, and there was the shock of being dragged through the door with her bare feet striking the cold ground.

I got my hand over her mouth and she bit me. I jerked it away and shook her. I asked, "What are you doing here?"

She must have recognized my voice. She screamed, "Playing house, you fool. Let me go. Paul! Paul!" I had hold of her left arm, but her right was free and she brought her hand down across my cheeks, fingernails digging four furrows from my temple down to my chin. "Get your gun," she yelled. "Paul, get your gun."

Rome didn't have anything on but a pair of drawers. He'd grabbed a shotgun and was running toward the door when suddenly I remembered I didn't have my gun. Just as Rome reached the door I gave Susan a push. Rome didn't have time to dodge. She plunged headlong into him and both skittered back through the door and I ran.

Just as I reached the corner of the building I heard the

shotgun boom. Rome had fired blindly into the night and I wasn't hurt, but the blast hastened my departure. I headed straight for the hotel, blood running down my cheek and from the finger Susan had bitten.

Effie patched me up, saying complacently, "Next time you'll believe me, I reckon." I didn't say anything, so she went on, "All that talk about you getting the dangerous end of the job was right, looks like. You got scratched and bit by the she-bear and it sounded like the he-bear harumpped at you after she got done."

Hardman and Logan came in, laughing so hard they couldn't talk. They had watched the show from the opposite corner of the store. We never did learn when Rome figured out that he had to get up on the roof and take the boards off the chimney, but by sunup they were gone.

19

JUDY'S PROMISE to meet me at the rock cabin made me feel like a small boy with a birthday coming up. I lived the day in my mind over and over; I thought of the things we would say to each other and of the things we would do, and I was in torment for fear that the weather would turn bad so she wouldn't come.

I got up earlier than usual Sunday morning and looking out of the window, saw that the sky was as clear as it had been for the past ten days. I built the fire and finished the chores long before Effie got breakfast. Then I had to sit fidgeting in the kitchen while Effie, wearing a white cap and a faded blue wrapper over her nightgown, poked around the pantry and kitchen in an irritating slow motion that made me want to yell at her.

"It ain't right for anybody to be as happy as you are on Sunday morning," Effie said as she poured the coffee. "You look like a robin in a garden full of worms."

"Just the good weather," I said in an offhand manner. "Thought I'd take a ride."

Effie returned to the table and sat down heavily. She gave me a penetrating glance, then she said, "If you don't git into a big hurry after breakfast, I'll fix a snack for you and Judy.

100

Chances are she'll never think of anything if she's half as excited as you are."

I ate in silence, humiliated at the ease with which Effie had seen through me. No one fooled her for very long. I waited impatiently while Effie fixed a sack of sandwiches and put in two big slabs of cake left from supper the night before. "Don't forget to fetch the sack back," she said tartly as she handed it to me.

I rode east directly toward the rim. There was no snow except in the foothills to the south, and on beyond, of course, where the high peaks reached for the sky and the pass between them was buried under thirty feet of snow. Maybe, as Russ Musil had said in the store, the pass would not be open until July. I wondered if I could stand that extra month.

The country tipped up as I approached the base of the rim. A number of dry washes cut through it at various angles, but as I came out of them, each ridge was a little higher than the one before. Cedars were larger and more numerous than I had seen them in any other part of the Hole. Judy's directions were scanty, and I began to worry about missing the cabin, but I was reasonably sure I was more than three miles from the O'Hara ranch, so when I reached the base of the wall I swung north, and within half an hour found the rock cabin.

Judy was not there. I was sick with sheer disappointment. Maybe O'Hara had found out what she planned and wouldn't let her come. Then I remembered I had left the hotel early and Judy had not set a time. I would wait, all day if necessary. I dismounted, and stripping the gear from my buckskin, staked him out in the clearing in front of the cabin.

A small spring bubbled out of the ground not far from the cabin to flow down the slope and disappear into the thirsty earth fifty yards away. I knelt down and drank. It was sweet cold water, and I wondered who had built the cabin and what its history was.

I went inside, expecting the interior to be dirty, a home for pack rats and spiders, the furniture gone or broken up, but I was completely wrong. The place was clean, as clean as any cabin with a dirt floor could be. The scanty furniture was intact: a bunk in the corner, two rawhide bottom chairs, a table, and shelves along one wall that held a number of cans with tight lids. The fireplace showed ashes of a recent fire, and when I examined the cans, I found they contained food in good condition. The rock walls were tight and well built, the sod roof in reasonably good shape.

I pondered this for a time, standing in the middle of the room, the door open. The cabin was being used by someone, and I wondered why Judy had asked me to meet her here. We were likely to have company. The thought left me a little sour, for I wanted to be alone with her and had expected to be. Then I wondered if she did not completely trust me, that she actually wanted someone else here.

I stood there a long time, so concerned with my worries that I did not hear her ride up. Her call startled me, and when I stepped out of the cabin into the sunlight, she had finished unsaddling and tying her pony. She waved when she saw me, saying, "I wondered where you were."

She was wearing a leather jacket and a dark green riding skirt, her broad-brimmed black hat held tightly to her head by a chin strap. She took off her hat as she came toward me, walking in her leggy, graceful stride. Suddenly I was a callow boy, wonderfully in love and struck dumb by her beauty and perfection of body.

She didn't stop until she was a step away, and then she stared at me as if puzzled. "What's the matter with you? Or is it me?"

I suppose I was red in the face. At least my cheeks felt as if they were on fire. I said, "I was admiring you. That's all."

"Thank you," she said. "I admire you, too." She thought I was joshing her, I think, for suddenly she stopped and bit her lower lip. "You meant that, didn't you, Bob?"

"Sure I meant it."

I saw the pulse beat in her throat and suddenly she brushed past me into the cabin. She said, "Don't, Bob. I'm nothing to admire. Not really. Don't forget I've got a hell-roarer for a father."

I followed her inside. "Effie says there's times when he's not unreasonable."

"She must mean when he's asleep," she said rebelliously. "Build me a fire, Bob. I'll make some coffee." Then she saw the sack on the table. "What's that?"

"Effie sent some sandwiches and cake. I didn't tell her where I was going, but she caught on."

Judy laughed, our moment of restraint gone. "Bless her old heart. But she didn't need to send anything. I always keep stuff here and cook a meal when I come."

"You mean you're the one who uses this cabin?"

"That's right. Nobody but me. It's been vacant as long as I can remember. Mike says it was built by an old hermit who lived here when the first settlers came. He just wanted to be let alone. Mike doesn't even know his name. I guess a lot of people in the Hole never heard of him or know that the cabin exists."

"How often do you come?"

"Almost every Sunday unless the weather's so bad I can't ride. It's like I told you the other day. Sometimes I think I'll go crazy, living with sheep and Mike and Dale Oren. Of course Dale is an improvement over Billy Wrangel." She turned away. "But you don't want to hear my troubles. Get me that wood."

I found an ax leaning against the back of the cabin and started on a dead cedar, not stopping until I had two armloads which I carried into the cabin and laid on the floor beside the fireplace. When I got the fire going, Judy, who had brought water from the spring, filled the coffee pot and set it on the fire.

For a time we sat in front of it, watching the flames curl up around the smoke-blackened coffee pot. I rolled a cigarette, then I said, "I'd like to hear about your troubles."

"Oh, I don't have any real trouble," she said. "I have good clothes and a roof over my head and enough to eat. Isn't that enough to satisfy anyone?"

I thought about it a long time before I answered. I considered my own lonely way of life, following cold trails, getting wet and chilled while I spent twenty hours at a time in the saddle. I had always taken pride in my toughness and self-sufficiency, but they were poor substitutes for the warmth and satisfaction a man gets from his own home.

Drifting years, wasted years except for the money I had in the Grand Junction bank. I hadn't known any better; I hadn't even given the future much thought. It had taken these months in Dirken's Hole to make me think about it. Maybe just meeting Judy O'Hara was what I needed to pinpoint it in my mind.

"No, it's not enough," I said with more feeling than I intended to show. "You've got a right to your own home and your children and a place in life that's yours and can't ever belong to anyone else."

"That's what I tell myself," she said. "That's why I come here. To be alone and dream like a silly girl. Of what I would have if I were a princess and had everything in the world right at my finger tips. So I cook a meal and lie on the bunk with the door shut, and for one afternoon out of a week I live in a dream world that's a long way from Dirken's Hole."

I sensed that she was talking to me in a way she had never talked to anyone else, that this was her one escape and that her troubles were far greater than mine. At least I could escape in June the first day anyone could get over the pass.

"Crazy, isn't it?" she murmured. "A grown woman acting like that."

"No," I told her. "Dirken's Hole isn't my notion of a place to live."

"Nor mine," she said. "It's mostly that I get all worked up inside. I don't have anyone to talk to. Maybe that's what's wrong. Lydia Smith is my best friend, but she never had a crazy thought in her head. She's too practical. Her life is Dick and her boys and the hard work of just keeping everything going. And Mike." She stopped, her face turning bitter. "The Lord decided Mike would be my father. I didn't. All he thinks about is the whiskey he makes and drinks and his sheep and being an important man in this little hole in the ground."

"Judy."

I reached out to take her hand, but she jumped up and lifting the coffee pot from the fireplace, took it to the table. "Bob, what's it like outside the Hole?"

She brought two tin cups and sugar to the table, then stopped to look at me. "Haven't you ever been outside?" I asked.

"Once that I can remember. It was when my mother was alive. I was ten. We went to Steamboat Springs. I thought it was a big city."

I got up and walked to her. "Judy . . ."

104

"Don't say it, Bob. I'm afraid. I'm terribly afraid. Don't spoil the nicest day I ever had. Just tell me what it's like outside Dirken's Hole. Leadville. Denver. Rock Springs. They're just names to me."

"You'll have to see them." She was standing on the other side of the table from me, forcing a smile. I asked, "What are you afraid of?"

"I don't know. Just what's ahead, I guess. I've been afraid ever since the night of the dance when I was so brazen that everybody in the Hole talked about it. I'm not like Russ Musil's daughter. Nancy lives the way a girl is supposed to. She'll marry one of Carter's cowboys and everybody'll give them a shivaree and they'll settle down on Skull and have a home and babies and I guess she'll be happy. But I can't do that. I'm that wild redheaded O'Hara girl who rides all over the Hole by herself, sometimes in the rain. Mrs. Carter and Mrs. Oren are always talking about me because I do things I shouldn't. Like having every dance with a stranger and scheming up a way so he could buy my basket at the Christmas party." She opened Effie's sack. "I'm hungry. Aren't you?"

It wasn't noon yet, but we ate Effie's sandwiches and cake and drank cup after cup of Judy's coffee, then I smoked a cigarette and when I finished it, I built up the fire. I came back to the table and sat down.

"Funny business here in the Hole," I said. "The people tolerate outlaws because they make money out of them, but they don't like them, so they go on with their own lives, ignoring men like Hardman and Logan if they can."

"That's right. But the funniest part of it is that some of the people aren't any better than the outlaws. Like Jesse Carter. He'd run every farmer off the creek if he could. If he owned the bottom land, he could raise his own hay and not buy it from Dick Smith and Russ Musil and the rest."

She looked at her hands, placed palm down on the table. She was plainly unsure of herself, and this surprised me because she had seemed exactly the opposite every time I had been with her. Then, eyes still on her hands, she asked, her voice low, "Bob, what was it you did that made them offer a thousand dollars for you?"

Without thinking about it except that I wanted to set her

right, I said, "Nothing. Those reward dodgers are a fake. I'm not an outlaw. I was sent here to find out who robbed the train near Rock Springs of fifty thousand dollars and wounded a trainman. I'm to take them out as soon as the pass is open."

"Hardman and Logan." She stared at me, her eyes suddenly filled with loathing. "Is that true?"

"Yes," I said. "Judy, I love you. I've been trying to tell you——"

She jumped up and ran to the door. I caught her just as she reached it and turned her around to face me. She was crying. She said over and over, "A bounty hunter! A bounty hunter!" To her it must have been the lowest thing a man could be.

"Listen to me," I said. "You don't understand. I've never done anything I'm ashamed of. I love you. I want you to marry me. I'll take you away from here as soon as I can."

"They'll hang you when they find out," she whispered. "They'll hang you and I hope they do. Now will you let me go?"

But I held her by both arms. "If you'd let me tell you how it is, maybe you'd understand."

"I understand what Jason Harwig is. Effie will kill you herself when she hears."

"I'm not like Jason Harwig. I never was."

I brought her to me by force and kissed her, but her lips were rigid against her teeth. When I let her go, she said, "Now I suppose you're satisfied. I had a right to be afraid. I guess I knew all the time how it would be."

She walked to her horse, saddled him, and rode away without a backward glance. I stood leaning against the rock wall of the cabin, not caring whether she told the truth about me to the Hole people or not. If she did, they would hang me just as she said, or Hardman and Logan would shoot me.

I just didn't care. It seemed to me that for one short moment I had held a little piece of beauty in my hands, a chance to be happy and to make Judy happy, but now it was gone.

20

I RODE to the rock cabin every Sunday in March, even when the weather was so bad I knew Judy wouldn't be there. Effie always sent a lunch with me, hinting that she'd like to know how my romance was progressing. I'd say everything was fine, giving her the impression I was seeing Judy every Sunday.

I didn't really expect her to show up, but I kept hoping. I was fully aware that I had made a great mistake when I'd told her why I had come to Dirken's Hole. I had spoken on impulse, not realizing how warped Judy's feelings were on the whole question of law enforcement. I should have, knowing Mike O'Hara. Besides, I had to admit that there was a difference between a bounty hunter and a lawman, a difference that would be hard to argue away.

One afternoon near the end of March I wandered into the kitchen of the hotel and sat down. Time hung heavily on my hands because it was a typical March day, blustery and cold with rain barreling down so hard we couldn't see the rim. Effie loved days like this when I'd sit and talk to her.

"You told me once that Mike was the main one who favored putting up with outlaws," I said. "Why?"

"He had some kind of trouble with the law before he came here. Then Billy Wrangel was wanted in three states. Murder in one state and a stage hold-up in another one."

"What about the third state?"

Effie scratched her fat nose, then she said hesitantly, "All I've got is a guess. Him and Mike ate dinner here one Saturday. They was purty drunk, and from what was said, I figured it was rape."

"And Mike kept Wrangel with Judy growing up?"

"That's what he done," Effie said. "But I will say this for Billy. He never done nothing out of the way all the time he lived here except beat the hell out of almost every man in the Hole. But for me, I'm glad he's dead."

After that I had less use for Mike O'Hara than ever. I was determined to see Judy again. She still came to the cabin, but always in the middle of the week. I had no way of knowing what day unless I stayed there all the time and I couldn't do that.

I always piled wood inside the cabin, and when I'd return the next Sunday, most of it would be gone and there would be fresh ashes in the fireplace. Finally, out of sheer desperation, I left a note for her, taking a chance that no one else would find it. I could think of nothing to say except that I loved her, that I had been there every Sunday in March hoping she would be there, too, and that she had been unfair to condemn me without giving me a chance to talk to her.

So I continued to hope. I was there in the rock cabin again the first Sunday in April, a rainy day but a warm one. Spring was here, real spring, and not the false promise of February.

I had trouble with the fire because she had left little dry wood, and the wood I brought in was soaking wet. But I finally got the fire going and piled more wood beside the fireplace so it would dry. Then I waited in the gloomy cabin, the door open, waited through one dreary hour after another while hope guttered out like a dying candle. Then she was there, standing in the doorway, water running down from her hat and off her slicker, standing and waiting like a child expecting punishment.

I said, "Judy," and held my arms out to her, and she ran to me. Her arms were around me and her lips welcomed mine, not the rigid lips I had kissed more than a month before, but warm and willing ones that told me more than words could ever tell me. When at last she tipped her head back to look at me, I saw that she was crying.

"Judy," I said. "Don't, Judy."

"I'm sorry, Bob. I just can't help it." She realized then that she was still wearing her slicker. "Oh, I've got you all wet. I'm sorry about that. I'm sorry about everything."

She unbuttoned her slicker and threw it and her hat on the table, and then she came to me again. This time I just held her, her head against my chest, and she seemed content to be that way while time ran on past us in uncounted minutes. Finally she stirred and drew away.

"Don't let your fire go out," she said. "I was here Friday and I used up almost all your wood. Then when it rained today I was afraid you wouldn't be able to get a fire started and you'd be cold."

"I guess just having you here is enough to keep me warm," I said.

She laughed shakily. "I was afraid you wouldn't come."

I piled more wood on the fire and we started a pot of coffee, then I took her hands. "Judy, will you let me talk now? Try to make you understand?"

"No. I'm going to talk first. I've fought you in my heart

108

almost from the first time we met. I don't know why I loved you but I did. And after that Sunday we were here together, I fought you even harder because I was so sure it would never work. I came every week and I knew you had been here on Sunday expecting to see me and you always left wood for me. Then after I read your note—well, I couldn't fight any longer."

"Why did you have to fight me?"

"Let's sit down in front of the fire. I guess I've got more talking to do than you have."

I brought a blanket from the bunk and spread it on the floor. We sat there, my arm around her, her head against my shoulder. She was silent for quite a while. I suppose she found it hard to start, but when she did, the words poured out of her.

"I've tried to think this out but it doesn't make much sense," she said. "I told you I was afraid. I've been afraid ever since my mother died. I was afraid of Billy Wrangel and sometimes I hated Mike because he kept Billy when he knew I was afraid. He talks as if he loves me, but he acts as if he doesn't love anything but his sheep. That's part of what doesn't make sense. I'm his daughter and sheep are—are just sheep."

"It makes sense with Mike O'Hara," I said.

"Now he lives with his ewes," she went on as if she didn't hear me. "They're lambing and he's losing a few lambs because of the cold and the rain. He gets so edgy he's not decent to me or Dale Oren. He's worked twenty pounds off Dale since he came to live with us."

She swallowed, and I felt her heart pound in her chest. She was like a wild, frightened bird that had knowingly flown into captivity. When I thought about the things she had done since I met her: running up the stairs of Rome's store to get help when I was fighting Wrangel, holding the shotgun on me when I brought Wrangel to O'Hara's ranch, eating the basket supper with me and showing no alarm whatever when Lydia Smith was scared ten feet away from her shadow, well, it didn't make sense she'd be frightened now.

"When I first met you at the dance," she went on, "you were like a breath of good clean air from outside. Even the air here in the Hole is dirty. Like Mike with his sheep. Jesse Carter acting so righteous when I know he was run out of

Middle Park years ago for rustling. Bud Stivers can't get a job in Wyoming because he was blackballed. Paul Rome's so greedy he'd let every family starve just so he can make a few more dollars."

She didn't mention Susan, but she must have thought about her, too, because she said, "Your father is different. I mean, he was when he came here, but the Hole's changed him. He's not the man I went to school to. I thought you'd be like him. Even when I heard you were a wanted man, it didn't bother me. I mean you weren't pretending to be something you weren't. All this time I knew I loved you, but I was afraid to let myself hope. I was afraid it would be like the rainbow, so pretty and sometimes so close, but when you reach out to touch it, it's never there."

My arm was hard around her, so hard it must have hurt, and now I was afraid, afraid in a way I had never been afraid before in my life, afraid that if I relaxed my grip and let her go, I would never have her again. All this time I had been thinking she didn't understand what the law was and I would have to explain it to her, but it wasn't that. It was the treachery every bounty chaser is guilty of some time or other, and I was as guilty as hell.

I had used my father as an excuse to come, I had made friends with the men I was to take to jail and they had saved my life. Now, if I took them in, I'd lose Judy. She had made that plain, in her indirect way. If a man was ever between a rock and a hard place, I was.

She had said her piece and it was my turn to defend myself, but there wasn't a damn thing I could say that would do any good. Instead of defending myself, I said, "You asked me what it was like outside. It's just the same as it is here except that you know these people too well. Outside you don't see it quite so plainly, but the greed and the brutality and the lies are there."

She said, "There must be love, too, and some tenderness."

"Sure there is," I said, "but you can find it here, too."

"I suppose so," she agreed doubtfully.

I had avoided the real question which I had to answer sooner or later, so I said, "About me. I've never done anything I'm really ashamed of. Until I came here, anyway. I never brought a man in who wasn't found guilty." She was silent and I knew that what I had said had not touched her. I tried again. "Judy, I can't undo what I've done, but I'll quit. We'll buy a ranch. I've got some money. We'll get married just as soon as we get to Steamboat Springs."

She was silent a long time. She didn't mention Hardman or Logan. I think it was the same with both of us. We couldn't bring ourselves to spoil this good and wonderful feeling that we shared.

Finally she said, "We can't leave together. You go first and I'll follow."

I said, "All right."

"Will you wait for me, Bob? Will you wait?"

"I'll wait forever if I have to. The worst part is that it's two months before we can get out. Or more."

"But there are a lot of Sundays between now and then." She tipped her head back and drew my mouth down to hers, and she said softly, "I'm not afraid, Bob. Not any more."

But I was. I was afraid of losing her. Hours later she rode one way and I rode the other, my buckskin slipping and sliding in the mud. I was not as happy as I should have been. The real issue between us had not been resolved. We had simply circled around it. We couldn't go on circling it, but for the life of me, I could not see any way to answer it. One way I would lose Judy, the other way I would lose my self-respect. That left a man no choice at all.

21

THE LAST of April turned dry and warm, as warm as most summers I had been used to in the higher altitudes. I didn't miss a single Sunday with Judy. I had never been happier in my life and apparently she felt the same. She showed none of the fear and reticence that had been in her the Sunday we'd made up. Instead, she was the eager, almost bold girl with whom I had danced last fall and liked so much.

When I mentioned it, she said, "You might as well get used to me, darling. When I'm afraid, I'm terribly afraid, and when I'm brave, I'm like a lion. Right now I'm not afraid."

All of this filled me with more love than ever for Judy. We made plans for hours at a time, discussing where we would buy a ranch, how big a spread it would be, what kind of house we would build, and how near a town we wanted to be. For my part, I favored the White River country, and I described it to her and told her about the town of Meeker.

So we lazed in the spring sunshine, and sometimes we dozed, or just lay in the grass that was beginning to turn green, my arm around her, her head on my chest. At times she would put her cheek against mine, or kiss me with all the fire I had ever dreamed I would find in a woman. Then she would lift her head and look at me, her moist, red lips slightly parted, and she would smile.

These were the beautiful, wonderful hours, like the passage across a placid river with the rapids just below. We could hear them if we listened, but we closed our ears. We never talked about them, but we knew they were there. Judy had to break with Mike. Effie would find out the truth about me. Somehow I had to make up with my father because I knew I would never see him again after I left the Hole. And then, of course, there were Hardman and Logan.

Strange how time runs out on a man. It seemed only a few days ago when I could say to myself that nothing had to be settled until the pass was open and that was months away. Now it was only weeks. With April warm and dry, Effie said, "You can look for a scorcher of a summer. It's my guess the pass will be open before the first of June."

I plowed Effie's garden and we got the seed in, but she shook her head and allowed we were wasting both our work and the seed. "If we don't get some June rains, that garden just won't do no good."

If time was running out for me, it had already run out for the farmers. A situation that had been bad for months became intolerable by the end of April. They had traded back and forth as much as they could. Effie gave them Saturday dinners on tick and even loaned them a little money, but it wasn't much help, having to pay the prices Rome charged.

They ate their hens, they butchered their sows, and the ones who were lucky enough to own a few head of beef cattle sold them to Jesse Carter for a fraction of what they were worth. Their resentment grew until it became a smoldering fire, but Effie said nothing would come of it.

"They'll get along until they cut a hay crop," Effie said.

112

"They just ain't the kind who'll take the law into their own hands."

"A bunch of old women," Hardman said derisively.

I made a point of staying away from both the store and the saloon. The truth was I disliked Rome so much after I had found Susan with him that I was afraid I'd kill him. But it would be murder, like stepping on a fat bug. It wasn't in me to kill a man who would not fight, and I knew Rome wouldn't.

Hardman and Logan reported to Effie and me everything that happened, how Dick Smith and Russ Musil and the rest of them would come in and practically grovel in front of Rome, but he'd tell them they were already in debt to him and he couldn't give them any more credit.

"What's the matter with the varmint?" Effie would rage. "Paul ain't smart, but he's got enough brains to know you can't get blood out of no turnip."

I thought he had an angle. Maybe Carter had made a deal with Rome to freeze the farmers out and they'd have to sell their land. Carter bought a great deal of hay. If he owned the bottom land along the creek, he could raise and cut his own hay for a fraction of what it cost him to buy under the present system.

When I told Effie my theory, she said, "Maybe you hit it. That fat toad would give his right leg to own the Hole."

It was bound to come to a head sooner or later, but I didn't expect it to work the way it did. I was cleaning out one of the corrals on a Saturday morning in early May when Logan ran around the barn. He said, "Come over to the store, Bob. Eli wants you to see the fun."

A number of rigs had driven into the settlement during the morning. I didn't expect trouble, but if there was, I wanted no part of it. I shook my head. "Effie won't like me walking out on her."

"She won't care," Logan urged. "Eli says he needs you."

"Eli don't need me," I said. "I'm staying here."

Effie was gathering eggs for an angel-food cake she was making for Sunday dinner. She came over to the corral and wanted to know what we were arguing about. Logan told her. She laughed and nodded at me. "Go ahead and give Eli a hand, Bob. He's just ornery enough to do the job. But don't take your gun."

113

"All right," I said, and leaning my fork handle against a corral post, I went with Logan.

When we reached the cottonwoods in front of the hotel, I saw there were more rigs tied on both sides of the road than I'd realized had come to town that morning. Another thing that struck me was the absence of the children. Usually when farmers came to the settlement on Saturdays they brought their families and, if the weather was good, made a sort of picnic out of it. The children would race up and down the road yelling like the wild Indians they were. But today it was quiet, and when I stepped into the saloon with Logan, the men were lined up along the bar, their sullenness a tangible feeling in the air.

No one was talking but Hardman who was telling one of his stories. I walked past him to the door that opened into the store and glanced through it. The wives were there, every one except Mrs. Carter who wouldn't belong here anyhow. They were lined up along both counters in twos and threes, talking in low tones or feeling the cloth of several bolts that Rome had placed on the counter for them. Mrs. Oren was among them, but when I glanced back at the men along the bar, I saw Dale wasn't there. Apparently the oldest boy had brought her in.

Rome was standing behind the dry-goods counter, the usual black stockings pulled up on both arms, his green eye shade on his forehead. His eyes were flicking from one group to another, and his face had a greenish hue that might have come from a bilious stomach or extreme fear. If it was fear, he didn't show it in any other way.

Suddenly Hardman pounded the bar with a fist. "Service, Rome," he bellowed. "Drinks for everybody." He threw a gold coin on the bar. "Hustle up, Rome. We're thirsty."

Rome hurried into the saloon, passing within a foot of me and ignoring me the way he had ever since I'd shoved Susan at him that night at his back door. "Sorry, gents," Rome said. He pocketed the coin and began setting glasses on the bar.

"Mighty slow," Hardman grumbled. "You ought to hire a bartender to take care of the Saturday business."

"Maybe I should," Rome agreed.

"Why don't you apply for the job, Sam?" Hardman asked.

"I'm thinking about it," Logan said, grinning.

As soon as Rome had served us, he said, "If you want anything, gentlemen, just call. I'd better get back into the store in case some of the ladies are in a buying mood."

He bustled out. Dick Smith said, "I notice he put the bottle back on the shelf."

"He's a businessman, Dick," Hardman said.

The air was stale and hot in the room, and reeked with the smell of sweat and Rome's bad whiskey. Dick Smith took a bandanna from his hip pocket and wiped his face. He said, "Hardman, we don't take kindly to your fun-making. I've been watching my wife and three boys starve for two months. For over a week we've been eating nothing but boiled wheat, and our wheat bin is damned near empty."

"Our friend Rome has been a mean, tight man" Hardman said expansively, "but he's about to have a change of heart."

Hardman moved back from the bar, took a hitch on his belt and walked into the store, motioning for Logan and me to follow. He stepped behind the counter and walked to where Rome stood. He didn't draw his gun. The women on the other side of the counter afterward said there was no intimidation whatever, but I was standing at the end of the counter and I saw him take a derringer out of his coat pocket and ram it into Rome's ribs. He didn't talk long, but what he said made Rome look more bilious than ever.

Rome motioned to Logan. "Call the boys in." They tramped into the store, as despondent a bunch of men as I had ever seen in my life. Rome cleared his throat, then cleared it again. "Ladies and gentlemen, you know this has been a severe winter, and the early storm last fall caught me with most of my supplies on the other side of the pass. But now we're having hot weather, so I judge the pass will be open soon and my wagons will be coming in again within another month. I feel that it's only fair to let you have anything you want, providing I can supply your wants, and I'll be glad to give you credit. I'll wait on this side, Logan." He swallowed, with an effort added, "Buel, you help out on the other side. And the prices will be what they were last fall."

I suppose it took thirty seconds for what he said to register, and then chaos broke loose. Everyone jumped to one counter or the other. I never worked harder in my life than I did for the next two hours. Flour, sugar, rice, coffee, tea, spices, crackers, and practically everything else were carried from the store in armloads to be piled high in the rigs outside.

On the other side of the room cloth was measured and cut from bolts at designated lengths. Shirts, pants, underclothes, shoes, even tobacco and shells flowed out in a stream. I estimated that more than a thousand dollars worth of merchandise went out of the store in those two hours. Even Hardman waited on customers, then Rome was busy for another hour checking the charge slips, initialing them at Hardman's suggestion.

When it was over and the last rig had rattled out of the settlement, Rome sat down in a chair in the back of the store. Sweat ran down his nose and dripped into his mouth. He swallowed, wiped his face with a sleeve, and swallowed again.

"Paul, you will be rewarded for what you done today," Hardman said genially, "but it probably won't be till you get to Heaven."

He had enjoyed himself this morning more than at any previous time since I had met him. Logan was grinning, too, but it had been Hardman's show and Logan had just followed along. But Rome found no pleasure in what had happened. His chin quivered as if he were a child who had been hurt but was resolved not to cry.

"Now Paul, don't take it like that," Hardman said. "Folks forget easy. They'll remember how big-hearted you were just now while they're eating their first square meal in months and chances are they'll forget what a mean son of a bitch you've been all winter."

Something happened to Rome then. I didn't understand it, but I saw it happen. His chin quit quivering. His face lost its greenish tinge, and an expression of concentrated hate took its place. I had never seen anything like it before in any man, and if I hadn't seen it myself, I wouldn't have believed Rome was capable of generating so much passion against anything or anyone.

"Hardman," Rome said in a low, even voice, "I'm going to kill you."

Hardman laughed, and motioned toward a rack of guns. "Pick out any of them six-shooters. We'll step out into the street and make it fair'n square."

"No, that would be suicide," Rome said. "I don't want to

116

die, but I'll kill you. I don't know how I'll do it, but I'm smarter than you are and I'll figure out a way."

Hardman winked at Logan. "He's smarter'n I am, he says. Maybe he's gonna kill me with a look. Or use his head."

Logan and I were already going out through the front door. Hardman followed, leaving Rome sitting there with his hands clenched on his lap. I said, "You'd better watch that bastard."

"Rome?" Hardman looked at me in surprise. "Aw, he's harmless."

"Maybe," I said. "Say, how did everybody happen to be here today?"

"Me'n Sam rode all over the Hole yesterday and invited 'em," Hardman said. "Everybody but O'Hara and Jesse Carter." He slapped Logan on the back. "Well sir, I guess we could get elected to any office we wanted if they had an election today. Robin Hoods! That's what they're calling us all over the Hole."

"You just said that folks forget mighty easy," I reminded him.

He shrugged. "What the hell! Let 'em forget. We had our fun."

He told Effie about it three times before the day was over, laughing so hard at times that Logan had to pick up the story. The real clincher came Monday when we heard that Jesse Carter had ridden the full length of the Hole on Sunday in his funny-looking buckboard, his wife beside him on the seat, and offered to loan all the farmers any amount of money they needed against the summer's hay crop.

Effie collapsed into a chair when she heard it. "Wouldn't you know it?" she gasped. "Wouldn't you just know it?"

22

IF APRIL had been unseasonably warm, May was unseasonably hot. We had a few showers, barely enough rain to prevent the garden from drying up completely. I kept the weeds down, but Effie didn't seem to care. She spent most of her time fanning herself on the back porch, telling me to "let the damned garden go." Then she'd look out across the floor of the Hole at the shimmering heat waves, and declare she'd never seen anything like it and she wouldn't last the summer out.

The snow line in the foothills to the south gradually receded and the creek rose until it was a thundering torrent. In most places on the level floor of the Hole it was high enough to swim a horse. A lake began forming in the north end where the creek ordinarily seeped away into the ground. I suppose the mysterious veins which conducted the water through the bowels of the earth simply weren't big enough to take care of this abnormal flow.

All winter I had fixed in my mind the important month of June. Then, as the snow piled up, I thought of July. So I kept putting off making any definite plan as to how I would take Hardman and Logan when the time came. The farmers who gathered in Rome's saloon on Saturday, everyone friendly now that the starving time was behind them, said the pass might be open the last of May, with the snow going off the way it was.

I was fully aware that I might wake up one morning to find my men gone. I assured myself that it didn't make much difference. Men like Hardman and Logan couldn't escape the law indefinitely. If I didn't get them, a lawman or Jason Harwig would.

Another fact was always in my mind. By letting them slip through my fingers, I would remove the last barrier between me and Judy. If I did, she would go with me anywhere, any time, and nothing Mike O'Hara could do or say would stop her. That was the way I wanted it. But something, and I could not identify it, would never permit me to let Hardman and Logan go. I suppose it went back to my childhood when my mother read stories to me and taught me to pray and talked about pride and honor and duty. I had promised Judy to give up bounty chasing, and I knew I could keep that promise, but this thing I had bargained to do I must do.

Somewhere Judy, maybe from her mother, or from her father, had picked up just as strong a conviction against deception as I had about keeping my word. I knew exactly how and what she thought. I was a modern Benedict Arnold, I had sold my saddle, I would not be a man she could trust if I took Hardman and Logan to jail. So every passing hour through the last of May added to my torment.

118

I did not risk discussing the question with Judy on the precious Sundays we spent together. I was haunted constantly by the fear that it was too good to last, so I fought to protect these perfect days. I would have the memories of them if nothing else.

But there was one problem I could talk to Judy about. I still had not been able to make up with my father. I saw him at a distance from time to time, hoeing in his garden to preserve the little moisture that was there, or going to the barn to milk, or sometimes just standing in his back yard in the evening staring at the sky. Even at a distance he seemed a little thinner and frailer than he had been the last time I had seen him.

Twice I went to his door and knocked. Both times Susan opened the door and looked at me with the utmost loathing, the kind of intense hatred that had been in Rome's face when he had looked at Hardman. I said, "I want to see my father," and then she shut the door and locked it. Once I tried to catch him when he was in the back yard, but apparently he saw me coming, for he turned and went inside.

Gossip always came to the hotel, from the store and saloon, or on Saturdays when our dining room was filled. My father, I heard, had resigned his teaching job. He could do nothing else, for the last weeks of the school term had been sheer anarchy. The talent that he'd always had with children had completely deserted him. There would be no party this time, no presents from parents in appreciation for what he had done for their children.

The school board had given my father no choice. He could live in the teacherage until fall, then he must go. I wondered if he had thought about where he would go or what he would do, and if Susan would go with him? Or would she, as Effie believed, leave the Hole with Paul Rome?

I talked to Judy about this, telling her everything back to the first day I had seen Susan just after my mother had died. Not that she could change anything. I just had to talk to someone who understood, and Judy did.

"Don't blame yourself, darling," Judy said. "I knew how it would be that very first night when you brought her to the dance and then gave me your attention. She wanted you. When she couldn't get you, she tried to destroy you. She's like a

119

killing frost in the fall. She destroys everyone who has anything to do with her, Link and your father—and she'll destroy Paul Rome."

The sooner she destroyed Paul Rome, the better. But meanwhile there was my father. I said, "I've got a queer feeling about Dad. When I was little, I was always in trouble. Fighting with some kid or other. Dad couldn't understand it. I think he was jealous of me. Maybe he thought my mother's love wasn't big enough for both of us."

"That's all behind you, Bob. It's what's ahead that counts. You've got to talk to him. If you don't, and he were to die, you'd always regret it."

"I've tried, Judy. What else can I do?"

"Catch him when he's milking. Or hoeing in the garden."

"The time and place have to be right," I said. "Out under the sun in his garden or in the barn when he's milking isn't."

She thought about that a moment and nodded. "I guess that's right. He's a strange man. I felt that when I was in school, even as young as I was. He's weak, the way you judge strength, but in other ways he's strong. I think you've underestimated him."

"Maybe," I said. "Susan, too, I guess."

"She's the one. You know, my mother was awfully superstitious. She believed in devils and angels and evil spirits. Sometimes I think she was right. Maybe Susan's haunted by an evil spirit and she can't help herself."

"Anybody can help himself," I said. "Otherwise nobody would be to blame for what he did."

"But the way she acts doesn't make sense. You've got to go over there and put your foot in the door and shove your way in. Hit her in the face and knock her out of the way if you have to."

I had felt like doing exactly that. When I rode home that evening, I considered it. Not much time left. Days. Possibly hours. I decided Judy was right. I'd force my way in. Somehow I'd make my father talk to me.

I did not reach the hotel until dusk. I was unsaddling in the barn when Effie came in. I thought she was going to scold me for being late, but she didn't. She walked along the runway to where I stood beside my buckskin. She said, "I milked, Bob." Then she came closer, but in the near-darkness of the

120

barn, her face was only a vague blob. "Your father's in the front room waiting to see you."

A sudden pain cut down through my middle, a sort of all-gone weakness. I had been working up nerve to force my way into his house, and now he was here. "I'll come right in," I said. I turned my buckskin into the corral and when I returned through the runway, Effie was gone.

The back door was open, lamplight spilling out across the porch and on to the yard. I went in, feeling the imprisoned heat of the day. Effie, her weatherbeaten face showing more concern than I had ever seen said, "Your supper's on the stove."

"Later," I said, and went on into the front room.

My father sat on the leather couch, straight-backed, his hands folded on his lap in a sort of feminine primness. He was as thin and frail as he had been, and the gray pallor I had noticed weeks ago was still on his face. But there was something else, too, a tenacious strength that was new. The thought struck me that at times dying men had this gift of strength, perhaps given to them to accomplish something they could not ordinarily have done. I wondered if that was true with him.

I said, "I'm glad to see you, Dad."

"I hoped you would be." He rose. "I want to talk, Robert."

"We'll go to my room," I said.

We climbed the stairs. When I lighted the lamp in my room, my father came in and I closed the door behind him. He looked around disapprovingly. Effie wasted no money in furniture. A cane-bottom chair, the bed, and a pine bureau that needed painting. That was all. No curtains on the window, no paintings on the wall, not even a calendar, and no rug on the floor.

He held out his hand to me. "Robert, will you shake hands with me?"

I took his hand, his grip firm, his eyes on my face, and I knew then he would not go away without our understanding each other. I knew, too, that in his own way he was a stronger man than I was. His coming here took courage that I would not have had.

He sat down on the bed. "This is a poor room, Robert. I'm sorry you could not have had the comfort of the spare bedroom

121

at the teacherage, but what is done is done. Now the room is being occupied. Susan has slept in it for some time."

I sat down in the chair and rolled a smoke. *He knows about Paul Rome,* I thought, and waited for him to go on.

"There is no substitute for courage," he said, "and no excuse for stupidity. I'm not going to ask you to forgive me. I just want to tell you what happened."

He got his pipe and tobacco sack out of his pocket, and his hands began to shake so that he spilled more tobacco on the floor than he was able to dribble into the bowl. He slipped the tobacco sack into his pocket, and sat there with the pipe in his hand, not lighting it for a time.

"I have often thought about your mother telling us we did not understand each other," he said, his voice holding none of the nervousness that was in his hands. "As long as your mother was alive, she guided me so I avoided the mistakes I would have made in dealing with people. After she died, I made them all. I told you my destiny was here. It is. I'll die here. I'm not yet fifty, but I'm an old man. I'm finished."

He said this as impersonally as if he were discussing the weather. I remembered Judy saying he had his own kind of strength and I was seeing it now. He lighted his pipe and then took it out of his mouth and let it go cold again.

"My success as a teacher was due to your mother. I did not know it when she died, but I realized it after I came here. I needed the little touches she managed so well. At Christmas, for instance. That is one reason I married Susan, thinking she could give me what I lacked. The other reason was that I was lonely and Susan pretended to love me."

He lighted his pipe again and pulled on it twice, then took it out of his mouth. "Even when I was young, I was never a capable man on the marriage bed, but fortunately your mother was not a sensual woman, so I was able to make her relatively happy. She had a great capacity for spiritual love, and she gave all of herself to me—and to you. I was not in any way equipped to marry Susan. I just hoped she would do at least a part of what your mother had done, but she couldn't. There was nothing but failure for us from the first night."

He tipped his head so I could not see his face. He said, "This is not an easy thing for a man to talk about, especially to his son."

122

"I admire your courage," I said. "Judy mentioned it today."

He glanced at me quickly, trying to smile. "Effie told me about you and Judy. I'm glad. I told you last fall she would make a good wife." He licked his brown lips, lowering his head, and went on, "The harder I tried to satisfy Susan, the worse it became. She taunted me about how it was when Link was her husband. Then you came, and—you'll remember that last night you were there, when I couldn't talk to you in the morning? Well, during the night she told me that you'd forced her that day and it was everything she wanted. I believed her. Don't ask me why. I was stupid, but you see, I couldn't ask you about it. I was afraid you would lie and I didn't want to make you lie. So you left, and then all during the winter she told me how she went to you. In the barn here at the hotel, and still I believed her."

He looked at me and for a moment he couldn't talk. Then he said in a trembling tone as if he were begging me to understand, "Do you see how it was? I wanted to beat you with my fists, but I couldn't. I wanted to kill you, but I couldn't. All I could do was to stay away from you and listen to her. Sometime, I don't remember just when, I began to suspect it was Paul Rome, not you she was going to. I followed her and spied on her. I waited back of the store and listened to them."

He could not look at me any more. He lowered his head again. "You don't know what it is to be sucked down into the quagmire of shame until it squeezes the very insides out of you and makes you an old man. I wanted to kill him, too, but I simply am not capable of killing a man, not even Paul Rome. And I was ashamed to come to you and tell you how I wronged you, so I let it drag on and on until now time is short."

If I had only understood. Or guessed. But this was an ugly thing, so ugly I had not believed even Susan was capable of doing it. I could only say, "I'm sorry. I wish I had made you tell me."

He stood up. "I'm to blame, Robert. Lay none of the guilt on yourself. I came tonight because this had to be made right between us. And I had to warn you. I don't know what they plan, but both Susan and Rome hate you, and Rome hates Hardman. They're going to do something to harm both of you, then they're leaving the Hole. I learned that much by listening at his back door." He hesitated, and then added vehemently, "I'm going to stop them, somehow."

I got up. I said, "Dad, I have to leave the Hole as soon as the pass is open, but I'll come back for you. And Judy. You'll live with us."

"Robert, Robert," he said, "I would ask for nothing better, but I won't be alive then. That's the way it should be."

We went down the stairs together and on out of the hotel. On the front porch I put my arm around his shoulders. All I could say was, "I'm glad you came. I feel better than I have for a long time."

"So do I," he said.

I stood on the porch and watched him disappear into the darkness.

23

THE FIRST of June fell on a Sunday, a fact that held some significance for me because it would be the last time I'd see Judy before I took Hardman and Logan out of the Hole. Nothing had changed between us. We still had failed to come to grips with the issue that we had purposely kept in the background.

Judy had never promised to marry me, but we both talked as if we took it for granted we were going to get married. I suspected that on Judy's part it was a question of what I did with Hardman and Logan. All I could do was to hope that Judy loved me enough to come to Steamboat Springs to meet me, once I had done the job I had come here to do.

I slept very little that Saturday night. I still hadn't hit on a plan for taking them. The pass was probably open now, although as far as I knew no one had gone out yet. Paul Rome said he expected his supply wagons in any day.

I knew that Hardman and Logan would kill me if they could as soon as I declared myself. So I lay awake hour after hour, turning and tossing, and trying to think, but accomplishing nothing. The upstairs bedrooms were ovens, never actually cooling off at night. Hardman and Logan had been sleeping outside for a week or more, then they'd come upstairs and stay in bed until nine or so, and after that they'd show up for breakfast.

None of Effie's barbed remarks about being lazy touched them. They just laughed at her and said they wouldn't be around much longer. Usually I didn't hear them climb the squeaky stairs, but this time it seemed I had barely dropped off to sleep when I heard them. I stayed in bed a few minutes, thinking about Judy, then I got up and dressed and went downstairs.

The morning was unbearably hot, even at this early hour with the sun barely above the eastern rim. I built the fire as usual and went outside, thinking I'd leave without breakfast if Effie wasn't up when I finished the chores. But when I came in with the milk, Effie had breakfast on the table.

We ate in silence, Effie grumpy because she hadn't slept well. "I'm going to close the hotel," she said. "If there's any snow on the pass, I'm going up there and lie in it till fall."

I got up as soon as I finished eating, tired of Effie's grumbling. I intended to shave and get started, but as I turned toward the dining room, I heard the front screen bang. I looked at Effie, wondering about it, certain it wouldn't be Hardman or Logan.

"There ain't no wind," Effie said as she rose. "Now who do you suppose that is?"

I didn't have time to make a guess, even if I'd wanted to. Paul Rome charged into the kitchen, his face paler than usual, his hair disheveled as if he'd just got out of bed a minute before. He tried to say something and choked, he swallowed and choked again.

"Out with it, man," Effie said testily. "What's the matter with you?"

"It's happened." Rome wiped a hand across his face. "It's happened. We've harbored these outlaws for years and it's finally happened."

"What's happened?" Effie demanded.

He backed through the dining room and on into the front room, looking around as if he was suddenly frightened. He asked in a hoarse whisper, "Where's Hardman and Logan?"

We followed him, Effie saying, "In bed."

Rome kept backing up until he reached the foot of the stairs. He wiped his face again. "Don't wake them till I get help," he said in that same hoarse whisper. "We'll hang them,

125

Effie. We can't keep outlaws out of the Hole, but we can show them they can't rob us."

"Paul, if you don't tell me what they've done . . ."

"They robbed my safe last night. Cleaned it out slicker'n a whistle. Come over and see for yourself."

"They took my money?" Effie asked incredulously.

"Yours and mine and O'Hara's and Carter's. They figure on getting over the pass today, but we'll show 'em. I'm going for help." He looked at me. "You'll keep them here till I get back, won't you? I can count on you, can't I, Buel?"

"No," I said. "They didn't do it."

"Who else but outlaws would know how to open a safe? And can you swear they were in their room all night?"

I couldn't of course. Since they were known outlaws, Rome would have no trouble pinning the robbery on them, but I knew it hadn't been them because they were too smart. They had enough money in their saddlebags to satisfy their needs and then some. Besides, as they had told me, they might want to winter here again some time.

"I don't know who else would do it, but they didn't," I said.

"So you're sticking up for them." Suddenly Rome seemed to notice something on the stairs. "Maybe you can explain this." He walked to the stairs and picked up a canvas money sack from the third step. He tossed it to Effie. "There's your proof. That came out of my safe. How would it get there unless Hardman or Logan dropped it going up to their room?"

"Oh hell," I said. "That's pretty thin. You could have left it there yourself when you came in."

"Somebody robbed my safe," Rome said doggedly, "but you claim I dropped the money sack. Are you accusing me of robbing my own safe?"

"It's the best idea you've had yet," I said. "It'd put money in your pocket and give you a chance to work folks up against Hardman and Logan. You're a dirty, crawling thing, Rome. Any man who would take my father's wife the way you've done this winter would do anything."

"Don't call me names," Rome said shrilly. "It isn't my fault if a man can't keep his own wife after he married her."

Effie was standing by the door, looking at Rome and then at me as if she didn't know what to believe. She had no more use for Rome than I did, and I didn't think she'd take any stock in his accusations. But her money was gone, too, and she knew more about Hardman's and Logan's records than I did.

"Let's go look at that safe," Effie said.

Rome didn't move. He was afraid of me. He couldn't keep from showing it, but still he stood there, clutching the money sack Effie had tossed back to him.

"You're in cahoots with them," he said. "I didn't think a Harwig man would do that."

"Harwig!" The word exploded out of Effie. "He's lying ain't he, Bob?"

"I'm not lying," Rome said. "Susan found a letter sewed inside his coat. It's from Harwig. Probably still in his coat if you don't believe me. He's a bounty hunter. Came here to get Hardman and Logan."

"He's got to be lying," Effie shouted hysterically. "Is he or ain't he?"

"Yes and no," I said. "I've got a letter from Harwig——"

Effie threw an oath at me and whirled to grab a rifle off a set of antlers on the wall behind her. She would have killed me before that wild burst of fury died, I think, but I didn't stand still to find out. I reached her in three strides and twisted the Winchester out of her hands.

"Stop it, Effie." I threw the rifle across the room. "Listen to me."

But the fury was still in her. Her lips curled away from her teeth. "You sneaking bastard, pretending you were a decent outlaw, eating off my table, taking my wages, and all the time you were working for that son of a bitch that shot my son."

"Shut up." But she wasn't ready to shut up. She started cursing me and I slapped her across the side of the face. "Sit down and listen to me."

I doubt that anyone had struck her since she was a child. The blow didn't hurt her, but it shocked her and she dropped down on the leather couch, wide-eyed, staring at me. Rome was edging toward the door. I wheeled in time to get him. I hit him on one side of the face and then the other. He spilled back against the wall and his feet went out from under him. He sat there, glassy-eyed.

"Tell her the truth," I said.

127

He was so scared he couldn't talk, or half knocked out, I wasn't sure which. I backed away so I could watch him and still talk to Effie. I asked, "You ready to listen now?" She nodded, and I told her exactly how it was, meeting the sheriff in Grand Junction and how he'd introduced me to Harwig. I ended with, "I'm not Harwig's man. When I agreed to come here, I didn't know how he'd shot Link. I aim to take Hardman and Logan to jail when the pass is open and I've promised Judy I'm done with bounty hunting."

Effie just sat there staring at me, her leathery old face showing no expression whatever. I asked, "Have I done anything wrong, Effie?"

She got up without a word and marched across the room to where Rome sat against the wall. She took hold of his shoulders and yanked him to his feet. "Let's go look at your safe."

He left with her, staggering a little. I stood in the doorway watching as they crossed the dusty road between the store and the hotel, Effie stalking along with her shoulders back. I wondered what Rome would do. Get word to Carter and O'Hara, probably. The farmers would fall in line, forgetting what Hardman and Logan had done for them a few weeks before.

"What's been going on?" Hardman called from the top of the stairs.

"Plenty. Get dressed. You and Sam are getting out of here."

"I ain't had breakfast yet." Hardman yawned. "Why should we get out of here?"

"Rome's safe was robbed and he's blaming it on you and Sam. He'll have every man in the Hole on your tail before night."

Hardman laughed. "I didn't think that rooster would cook up a deal like that." He yawned again. "Maybe we had better get dressed."

"I'll get your breakfast," I said, and went into the kitchen.

It came to me clearly then, the whole pattern. Susan hated me and Rome hated Hardman, Logan, and me. They'd planned this to get all three of us. Rome had expected Effie to kill me. Or at least pull her over to his side and make a fugitive out of me along with Hardman and Logan. This must have been what my father had heard Rome and Susan discussing when he'd listened at the back door of the store.

No one would believe Rome had robbed his own safe. The more I thought about it, the worse it stacked up. All winter I'd heard how the Hole people held together against outsiders, how they tolerated the outlaws but didn't like them. Now the truth was out about me and I might be worse off than either Hardman or Logan.

I was frying eggs when Hardman and Logan came into the kitchen. Hardman yawned, scratching under his left arm, then along his ribs, and finally his head. He sat down and yawned again. "Well, Bob, is this the day the great bounty hunter takes us over the pass?"

I almost dropped the spoon I was holding. If I made a motion for my gun, I'd be a dead man. I turned around slowly. "Did you hear what Rome said?"

"No." Hardman yawned again. "Hell, man, we've known all the time who you were. Why, there ain't a rider on the owlhoot between here and Montan who don't know about Bob Buel. Where do you think we've been all our lives?"

24

I DON'T know how long I stood there staring at Hardman. Logan was openly laughing. I was sure Hardman was amused, too, but he was like a man grinning at you from behind a brush pile.

"Hey." Logan motioned toward the stove. "You're letting our eggs burn."

"Tend to your business, cook," Hardman said. "I hate burned eggs almost as much as I hate cold eggs."

I had to turn my back to them. A prickle worked up and down my spine. I was scared, as jumpy-scared as I had ever been in my life. All winter I had been assured by the certainty that I knew who they were, but they didn't know who I was, an asset that balanced off their advantage in numbers. Now I realized I had been on quicksand all the time.

Confidence began returning to me. They'd had all winter to kill me, so it wasn't likely they'd force a fight now. I took their eggs to them, poured their coffee, and dished up two bowls of oatmeal mush from the pan on the back of the stove. Then I sat down at the table and rolled a cigarette.

"Why did you boys let on all winter you didn't know me?" I asked.

Hardman winked at Logan. "It looked like a mighty dull winter. We figured to liven it up some." He took a bite of egg, and some of the yolk, still runny, remained on his lower lip. He scraped it off, drank his coffee, and put the cup down. "Me'n Sam argued over it some. He wanted to plug you just to be safe, but I says, 'No, it's a sporting proposition, and we're a pair of sports.' I took you for a good man, all right, but we're good men, too, and there's twice as many of us. I've been right curious about how you was gonna handle this."

"You've got a chore on your hands." Logan reached for the sugar bowl and dipped out three heaping spoonfuls for his mush. "Any way you cut it, you've got a chore."

They kept their hands in sight. I could have gone for my gun and maybe got one of them, but the other one would have got me. I wasn't one to take long chances. It was the same with them. So, after considering it a minute, I breathed easier. We weren't going to have any trouble right now, but when we did, I'd have my tail in a crack and a squeeze on it.

"Looks like I played it wrong," I said, "but Harwig figured that if he hadn't heard of me, you wouldn't, either."

"Harwig's lucky it wasn't him. If it had been, I'd have plugged him the day he rode in here." Hardman leaned back in his chair, took a cigar out of his pocket and bit off the end. "Harwig's a back-shooting bastard, but you've got a good reputation. Guts enough, but fair. That's why I figured it'd be fun to play along."

I thought I heard Effie come into the hotel, but I listened a moment and decided I'd been wrong. I said, "That's the way I feel about you boys. Hell of a note, isn't it?"

Hardman lighted his cigar and blew out a long plume of smoke, the picture of a perfectly contented man. "Sure is. Just what are you going to do about it?"

"Nothing right now." I shook my head as I thought about the past winter. "You even propositioned me to throw in with you."

Hardman laughed. "We sure snickered over that fake reward dodger. Alias the Ochoco Kid! Hell's fire, Harwig don't give us credit for being smart enough to carry slop in a bucket." He pulled on his cigar again. "But about joining up

130

with us. If you'd said yes, we'd have knowed you was going to try to get the drop on us when we got over to the other side, say around Steamboat Springs. But you were honest, so we figured we'd play along some more."

Again that prickle down my spine. If I had given the wrong answer that day, I'd have been a dead man. I wasn't sure I was far from it right now. Logan was still grinning, but there was no reading Hardman's face. I remembered how often I had noticed that his laughter never reached his pale eyes. Cool and tough, I thought, and deadly.

I said, "I've had trouble with Judy on account of you boys. She doesn't want to marry a man who thinks he has to take two men to jail who saved his life."

"I've seen duty bust better men than you," Hardman said.

Logan asked. "You told her who you are?"

"Yes. Why?"

"I was wondering how she found out. That damned Susan knowed all the time, but she didn't want it to get out yet. She told Rome, though, and after we smoked 'em out that night, Rome let it slip to us, figuring we'd take care of you."

Hardman laughed. "We thanked him proper. I reckon he's wondering why you're alive."

"He told Effie this morning I was a Harwig man," I said. "I guess he thought she'd plug me."

"He's a real genywine, ten-carat bastard." Hardman studied his cigar a moment, and added, "If you ever see Harwig again, tell him he's a fool. He should of knowed we'd heard of you. Any man who listens to the leaves rustle can tell you all about every lawman and bounty hunter between Montan and the Rio Grande. I don't mean the politicians who get elected sheriff and the piddling town marshals, but if a man amounts to a damn, we've got him pegged."

"Take a good look at us," Logan said. "Are we any worse than Harwig?"

Before I could answer, Hardman went on, "I've been in this game for twenty years, except for the time I was in Deer Lodge, and I never killed a man on a job. Everybody's got his notions of what's right and wrong. Me, I figure it ain't wrong to rob a train or a bank."

"We aren't going to convert each other," I said. "Right now you're in a jam."

Hardman dismissed Rome with a gesture of contempt. "I ain't worried about nobody in the Hole but you."

"You can forget me for right now," I said. "You've got to get out of here. I don't want the hotel shot up and a lot of men killed who don't deserve it."

Effie came in through the dining room and sat down at the table. She said, "Now ain't this a hell of a mess?"

"Oh, I dunno," Hardman said. "We ain't scared."

"You'd better be," Effie said. "I finally got it through my thick skull that Bob's right. Rome done it, but everybody else is gonna think it was you boys." She scratched an ear. "Where do you suppose Rome hid it?"

"Probably in the building," I said. "Maybe his kitchen or bedroom."

"No, he's too slick for that," Effie said. "When Carter or O'Hara gets here, I'll make 'em look, but I don't figure we'll find anything. Well, you boys have got to ride."

"We ain't budging out of this hotel," Hardman said. "What's the matter with you?"

She stood up and glared at them, her hands on her hips. "Oh yes you are if I have to run you out myself. I'll stake you to grub and I'll swap horses with you if you need it, but I ain't gonna have this hotel shot to flinders."

"Aw, we'll throw a little lead and they'll run like rabbits," Logan said.

"No they won't," Effie snapped. "Rome's gone to Oren's place. He's gonna send the oldest boy after the farmers and he's gonna fetch Carter and his crew. He sent Susie after O'Hara. The whole kit and kaboodle will be here by dark and they'll start after you."

"There'll be twenty of them," I said. "Figuring each of you is worth three or four of them, you're still outnumbered."

Hardman dropped his cigar stub into his coffee cup and got up. "Sam, it gravels the hell out of me to run, but they're talking sense."

"Sounds like it," Logan agreed.

Effie was in the pantry. She called, "I'll fill a flour sack with grub for you."

Hardman asked, "Where'd you think we'd best head?"

"North," Effie answered. "Get up on that bandit trail as far as you can. From one of them ledges you can see all that

132

end of the Hole. If they get snibberty, you can fan their ears with a little lead."

"I've got a better idea," I said. "You know that rock cabin east of here, Effie?"

She poked her head out of the pantry. "Yeah, but I sure had disremembered it. I'll bet there ain't three men in the Hole who know about it."

"It's tight," I told Hardman. "If they pin you down, you can hold off an army. There's a spring close to it, and grub inside the cabin. Cut plenty of wood in case you have to hole up."

"How'd you know so much about it?" Logan asked.

"I've been meeting Judy there," I said.

Hardman was looking at me intently, brushing a finger down one side of his mustache and then the other. He said, "Bob, if you get into a tight with this bunch today, me'n Sam won't be around to bail you out. Maybe you don't know it, but they don't like you much."

"I know it," I said, "but I don't aim to get into a tight. I'll try to talk to them. That's all."

"There's one little angle I can't figure," Hardman said. "You could collect for our scalps whether you fetch us in alive or not. Why don't you just let 'em hang us?"

Effie was watching me intently, her lower lip jutting at me in that peculiar way she had. I knew that what I said now would make all the difference in the world in the way she felt about me.

"Eli," I said, "you told me once there were two kinds of polecats you couldn't stomach, dry-gulchers and crooked gamblers."

"Yeah, but what's that got to do——"

"That's the way I feel about lynching," I said. "They aren't going to hang you."

I satisfied Hardman, but I wasn't sure about Effie. Hardman and Logan went upstairs to get their things. When they came down, Effie gave them the sack of food. I said, "Judy will be at the cabin some time today. Tell her what happened and send her here."

"That ain't so smart," Effie objected. "We don't know what's gonna happen."

"She can't stay at the cabin," I said, "and I don't think she ought to go back home."

Effie sighed. "All right, send her here."

I went outside with Hardman and Logan, and a few minutes later they were riding east toward the rim. When I returned to the hotel, Effie was sitting at the table staring into space. She was sweating, and some of her hair dye had started to run down the side of her face.

"Bob." She swallowed, and started to say something, and swallowed again. Then she shouted at me, "Damn it, I'm sorry I tried to kill you a while ago."

It was the nearest to an apology I had ever heard her make. I said, "Forget it, Effie," and let it go at that.

25

THEY BEGAN coming in the middle of the afternoon. Russ Musil was the first, then Dick Smith, and not long after that Jesse Carter showed up with Bud Stivers and most of the Skull crew. Paul Rome rode with them in the painful manner of a man who was not used to the saddle and had already been there too long. The rest of the farmers straggled in, but I didn't see Mike O'Hara.

I watched for Judy from noon on, but it was almost four when she rode into the yard between the hotel and the barn. I was cleaning out the henhouse when I saw her. I threw the hoe down and ran through the squawking hens to where she had pulled up her pony.

I held up my arms and she swung out of the saddle into them: I kissed her with violence that had accumulated in me from almost four hours of waiting. When she was finally able to push me back, she held me at arm's length, her blue eyes bright with laughter.

"Are you that glad to see me, Bob?" she asked.

"I'm more than glad," I said. "This has been a day."

"I know, I know," she said.

"Judy, promise to marry me. Promise that no matter what happens today, you'll marry me."

For a long time we stood that way, my arms still on her shoulders, her hands against my chest, and she was looking at me as if trying to measure our love, to see if it was enough

134

to take us through the years that waited. The laughter was gone from her eyes now, and suddenly there were tears.

"I promise," she said. "I'll marry you, if you'll have me, no matter what happens today or tonight or tomorrow."

"You go on in," I said. "Effie's over at the hotel. I'll put your horse up."

I unsaddled her pony and left him in the corral with my buckskin, then I emptied the wheelbarrow and put it and the hoe away, leaving the rest of the drop board dirty. When I went in, Judy was standing at a window in the front room, looking at the store across the street.

"What happened today?" she asked. "After Hardman and Logan left?"

"Nothing. The crowd's still coming."

"What will they do?"

"Rome will try to make a lynch mob out of them," I said. "It's the only way he can protect himself. After the crowd hangs two men, it's got to believe they were guilty. Later on nobody's going to think anything about it when Rome leaves the country with the money stashed away in his carpet bag."

"You talk as if you'd seen it happen."

"I have. I'm not going to let it happen here."

"One man against twenty," she said, "but I believe you can do it."

"With some help from you and Effie." I thought about it a moment, and added, "Isn't that something? The only two people I can count on in the whole valley are women."

She was looking at me so intently that I glanced away. It was almost as if she had never seen me all in one piece before. She said, "Bob, I've always thought, and I suppose it's because Mike taught me to think that way, that bounty hunters didn't think about anything but money, like men used to bring in Indian scalps for so much apiece."

"You're wrong," I said. "With me anyway."

She turned to look out of the window again. "I would have been here sooner, but I stayed to talk to Hardman and Logan. Hardman said they told you this morning they'd known all the time who you were, and if you'd been a jumpy man, you'd have gone for your gun and they'd have killed you."

"If I'd been a jumpy man," I said, "I'd have been dead a long time ago."

135

She nodded as if she understood that. She said, "Don't get mad at me, but I promised them you wouldn't take them in."

"You promised!" I grabbed her shoulder and shook it. "Don't make promises for me. You understand?"

"I understand," she said, "but you don't. I don't like Hardman and Logan. They've got to be captured and put in prison. I know that. They're not Robin Hoods. Not really. They just like to think of themselves that way. I mean, Hardman didn't make Rome give credit because he felt sorry for the farmers. He was just having fun."

She turned and put her hands against my chest, hard, brown little fists that pressed against me. "Bob, try to understand what I'm saying. If you were a lawman, I wouldn't argue with you. But you aren't. You took this job for money. There's a difference. I love you, Bob. I love you very much. I don't want you killed."

What could I say to that? I looked at her, feeling utterly helpless. I couldn't really argue with her. Still, I had made a bargain last fall. That was the only part she didn't understand, how I felt about giving my word.

Effie came in, and Judy dropped her hands and turned from me, asking, "How are you, Effie?"

"I ain't good," Effie grumbled. "By God, this has been a day to remember. Yesterday I had four thousand dollars tucked away in Rome's safe. Today I don't have a nickel." She dropped down onto the leather couch and spread out as if she had suddenly wilted. "Judy, I came near fixing it this morning so you wouldn't have no husband. I tried to shoot Bob."

This was something Judy hadn't heard. She stood there, shocked, staring at Effie in horror. I said, "Quit it, Effie. I told you to forget it."

"I can't. I came so near falling into the trap Rome laid that I get the creeping shivers every time I think of it." She waved a hand toward the store. "Now all them fools, Jesse Carter and all of 'em are running after Rome like a bunch of calves with their tails up. I made Jesse go over Rome's kitchen and bedroom and parlor with me, and we hunted all over the store and saloon, but we didn't find nothing. Where do you suppose that devil hid the money?"

"I don't know," I said, "but he'll cave if we get a little pressure on him."

Effie mopped her face with a dirty handkerchief. "We ain't in no shape to put any pressure on him, not with Jesse and Bud Stivers and all of 'em backing him up."

"Do they know Hardman and Logan are gone?"

"Sure, and they're cussing you for it." She scratched her right thigh and then her left one. "I dunno how you're gonna come out. I'm a little scared of it."

"He can leave here," Judy cried. "He can go to the cabin with Hardman and Logan. He doesn't owe anybody in the Hole anything."

"No sir, he don't," Effie said, "but I've got to know this boy purty good. You're getting a man, Judy. If he's what I think he is, he ain't gonna walk out. Not yet."

"Why?" Judy demanded. "Just tell me why."

"It's got something to do with the way he's put together," Effie said. "You tell her, Bob."

"I made a promise, Judy," I said. "I told Hardman and Logan they wouldn't hang."

"Not for something they didn't do anyhow," Effie said, "and they sure didn't do this one. The more I see Rome cavorting around, the more I know he's our bird."

"Are they going after Hardman and Logan?" I asked.

"Not till Mike gets here. There ain't no real leader there yet. Mike'll be it. Right now they're working up their courage and Rome's giving it away by the bottleful. That's the tipoff if they had sense enough to see it. Imagine Rome giving anything away." Effie wiped the sweat off her face again. "Judy, do you feel like getting supper?"

"Of course I'll get it."

"There's a pie in the pantry," Effie said. "And some o' that roast beef left from last night. We'd better eat it 'cause it won't keep in this weather."

When Judy left the room, Effie motioned for me to sit beside her. She said in a low voice, "It's a good thing you ain't been over there today. You couldn't have done no good, but maybe you can later tonight. Mike's the one who's gonna think of that cabin. When he does, they'll light out for it. Somebody's got to get there before they do and warn 'em. Maybe Judy can."

"What good can I do?" I asked. "Now or later?"

"I ain't sure," she admitted, "but I know it's gonna take a turn as soon as Mike gets here. They'll hunt this Hole from one end to the other. Hardman and Logan can't go nowhere except up there on that bandit trail where they can fort up and see all that end of the valley. If there's a siege, they're whipped 'cause there ain't no water on that trail, but it'll give 'em some time. Our only chance is to turn this whole business against Rome."

"We can't do that till they get mighty tired of running and chasing," I said.

"We'll see." Effie patted me on the leg. "Go give Judy a hand with supper."

I left her sitting there glowering at the floor. Suddenly I thought of my father. This was the thing he was going to stop, but what could Thomas Buel, a man of books, do against everybody in Dirken's Hole?

26

AFTER SUPPER Effie said, "I'm going back over there. Rome's got the bit in his teeth and he's running good, but maybe I can grab his ankle and drop him on his butt." She looked at me speculatively a moment. "After Mike shows up, you'd better come over for a while. They all know now you're a man-hunter and not an outlaw. They might listen to you."

"I'll come with him," Judy said.

"You stay here," Effie said sharply. "Better get your pony saddled up, too. If Mike happens to make the right guess, you're gonna have to high-tail to that cabin and get Hardman and Logan moved."

"Effie," Judy said. "Effie, I've . . ."

She stopped, embarrassed, and Effie said impatiently, "Say it, girl, say it."

"I've dreamed a lot of crazy dreams," Judy said, staring at the floor. "Like dreaming about a man coming to the Hole who would love me and I'd love him and he'd take me out of here. And he did come." She lifted her head in the proud way she had and looked defiantly at Effie. "Now you want him to go over there and get shot. Or have him shoot Mike. That would almost be as bad."

"Judy girl." Effie put an arm around Judy's waist, the only show of affection I ever saw her make. "He's a good man. You ain't gonna lose him. Not if I can help it. But this here is a mess. Rome's gonna make widows out of some women and orphans out of a lot of kids the way he's working, and I ain't gonna stand around and let him do it if I can help it." She looked at me. "Don't fetch your gun when you come."

She started toward the dining room. I said, "Effie, when this is over, I've still got to take Hardman and Logan out of here."

She was silent for a moment, her face shadowed in the gathering twilight. "That's between you'n them and I ain't butting in, but I'm hoping you make it. I learned something today I should have known a long time ago. If I had, Link might be alive today. Sooner or later we've got to fix it so Dirken's Hole ain't no outlaw hideout."

She tromped out. When the screen door slammed, Judy said, "I'm scared, Bob. I'm not a lion any more."

"You will be when the time comes," I said.

I had already brought in the milk. Judy strained it and then I helped her with the dishes. After that we saddled her pony and my buckskin and left them at the back door so they wouldn't be seen from the store. I filled my canteen and dropped some of the roast beef and a few biscuits into a sack and tied it behind my saddle.

"The moon's almost full tonight," I said.

"We may need it," she said.

"I guess you know the Hole as good as anybody."

"Better."

"If you have to run for it, you could take them on quite a chase, couldn't you?"

She laughed. "I could run their tails off. I know every sheep and game trail there is."

"I'm going to head north," I said. "People see things different in the daylight. After a few hours of riding, they'll get the whiskey jolted out of them, then maybe they'll listen when they won't listen now. A lynch mob's a funny thing. Takes whiskey and time and a lot of egging on, but after it reaches a peak, the cussedness begins working out of them."

We went back into the hotel and I dragged the leather couch around so we could sit on it and watch the store from the window. The room did not cool off as darkness came on, but

139

I thought we were better off here than outside on the porch. So we sat there, holding hands, while the last scarlet banner of sunset died above the western rim and the moon tipped up over the eastern wall. Some night bird was calling from one of the cottonwoods, and a cricket under the porch started singing.

An hour passed, and then two. We didn't talk. I don't know what Judy was thinking about, but my mind went back to that cold day when I had ridden over the pass and into the Hole, and I thought how different it was from these last scorching May days, how everything had tied in together, how the people and the things they had done had formed a pattern. The big men, Carter and O'Hara and Rome, and the little ones, my father and the farmers, and the thread of evil that Susan had woven through that pattern right from the beginning. Only Effie and Judy seemed to stand apart.

I thought of Sam Logan and I wondered what had made him the man he was. Hardman was different, for he went back to another generation, but Logan was my age and in many ways we were alike. But his destiny had led him one way and mine another, a destiny that had been shaped at birth, or perhaps at the very moment of conception. That brought me to my father, and it jarred me out of the past into the present, to my father's fatalistic conviction that he was to die here.

I felt it was what he wanted, what he would actually seek, and I remembered him saying that shame had made an old man out of him. I understood how that could be, the agony that must have been in him for months, knowing that any other man would have sought violent revenge but he could not. Something came to me that had escaped me before, that his gentleness had been a virtue in all the other places where he had lived, but here it was a weakness that had trapped him.

Judy squeezed my hand. She whispered, "Look."

A man had just ridden by. The door of the saloon was open, and when he went in, the light was upon him and I saw it was O'Hara. I thought how much like him this was. He would not be diverted when there was work to be done, but he would take the time now that it was dark to attend to another chore, confident that he could handle it in a few hours and then go back to his sheep.

I got up. I said, "Time to go." I took off my gun belt and

left it on the floor at the end of the couch a few inches from where my rifle leaned against the wall. Judy was on her feet, too, but she didn't say anything for a full minute. She was breathing hard as if she had been running, then she said, "I'll wait here," and I left the hotel.

I had given this some thought, and I was convinced that the only thing I could do was to divide them along the natural line of cleavage, the farmers on one side, O'Hara, Carter and Rome on the other. When I stepped into the saloon, Rome was working behind the bar, his round face glistening with sweat. Tobacco smoke ribboned over the heads of the men, and the smell of it mingled with the odor of cheap whiskey and the stink of too many unwashed people in too small a room.

For a time I stood there unnoticed. I was surprised to see my father sitting alone at a table, a spectator to what must have been a strange scene to him. Most of the men were standing at the bar, a few in a little circle in the middle of the room. Effie was with them, and then I saw Susan near the door that led into the store. Pretty, as pretty as sin, in a dark green riding skirt, a yellow blouse, and a red neckerchief. She had color, if nothing else.

No one seemed to pay any attention to me as I moved around the wall to my father. I said, "You can't do any good here. You'd be better off home."

Not that it was any of my business. I didn't think he wanted advice from me, but he was alone, terribly alone, and I knew he'd get hurt when the blow-up came. He looked at me gravely and shook his head, and I saw he was not offended.

"I've got to stay here," he said doggedly. "If they go after Hardman and Logan, I've got to ride with them."

I moved back to the door, feeling I had done all I could. In any case, I would not have tried to persuade him to do anything but what he felt he must. Perhaps he would find what he sought from these people, and if it was what he wanted, I was not one to argue with him about it.

I didn't think Susan saw me when I first came in, for her eyes were on Rome, but now she did. For a moment our eyes met through a lane between the men at the bar and the circle in the middle of the room. She smiled, a provocative smile, and straightened her shoulders, tightening the tips of her firm breasts against her blouse. I had a feeling she was trying to

141

tell me that everything would have been different if I had been the one who had taken her instead of Paul Rome.

Suddenly O'Hara's great voice boomed out, "Will somebody tell me why you've all been standing around getting drunk and wasting the whole day?"

"Hardman and Logan won't get out of the Hole," Carter said, "so we waited on you."

"All right, I'm here. Effie says they ain't in the hotel. Jesse says he's got this end of the pass covered. Now it stands to reason they ain't in the bottom along the creek. They'll head for the rim somewhere, maybe this end of the bandit trail where they can fort up. Anybody got a better idea?"

Apparently no one had, so O'Hara went on, "We'll split up. Jesse, you take half the boys and I'll take the rest. We'll go east till we hit the rim, then I'll swing north with my bunch and you go south. We'll pick up their sign somewhere and flush 'em into the open."

"And we'll hang them," Rome shouted. "We'll pull them up and down by the neck until they tell us what they did with that money and then we'll hang them for keeps."

I should have left before then. I couldn't do anything more than my father could. Not with men who'd drunk as much whiskey as they had and been egged on as they had by Rome. But I had waited too long. Now Susan's strident voice rose above the rumble of the crowd, "Maybe the great man-hunter can tell us where to look."

They glanced at her and she motioned at the door, and that focused their attention on me. Too late. I couldn't back out now. Rome shouted, "If he'd kept them in the hotel like I told him to, we'd have them, but now we've got to ride to hell and back hunting them."

"How do we know he's a man-hunter?" Susan demanded. "Maybe that reward dodger was right. Maybe he's thrown in with Hardman and Logan."

They started moving toward me like a wall of water just breaking through a dam, the rumble that rose out of a dozen throats more of an animal sound than a human one. I grabbed an empty whiskey bottle off the bar by the neck and held it in front of me.

"I'll crack the first skull that gets offered," I said. "I left

142

my gun in the hotel so you'd know I didn't come here to kick up a row, but you don't seem to be able to see or think."

"You kind o' tired, Buel?" It was one of Carter's cowboys, more drunk than the rest. "You been with Judy O'Hara most of the day, ain't you?"

I started toward him, but O'Hara was closer. He hit the man just once, squarely on the point of the chin, the sound of it like that of a meat cleaver on a piece of beef. The cowboy went back, sprawled across a table, and rolled off to the floor. He lay face down and didn't move.

"Thanks, O'Hara," I said. "If the rest of you aren't as drunk as that bastard, you'd better do some listening. I aim to take Hardman and Logan to jail for a train robbery they pulled off last fall. They can answer to this charge, too, and stand trial, but you're not going to hang them."

"Listen to him," Susan jeered. "He's in with them, right up to his neck."

If it hadn't been for my father, I would have told them what had been going on between Susan and Rome, but he had suffered enough, so I ignored her. I saw Effie was edging toward me and I wondered if she had a gun.

"You'd better listen to me," I said. "Smith. Musil. The rest of you hay-raisers. Who fixed it so you and your families didn't starve? Hardman and Logan, in case you've forgotten, and now you want to hang the men that fed you. Well, you'd better hang the man who robbed you all winter."

"I won't listen to that," Rome yelled. "I fed you. I'm the one who gave you credit."

"You boys know why he got generous?" I asked. "It's because Hardman shoved a derringer against Rome's ribs and changed his tune. And who rigged the deal with Rome? Jesse Carter, that's who. As soon as he found out the deal was off, he went around so sweet honey wouldn't melt in his mouth offering to loan you all you needed. He was trying to use Rome to get your land, and if you had any kind of a brain between your ears, you'd know it."

They started for me, Carter and Stivers in the lead, the rest of the Skull hands following. I swung the bottle and knocked Stivers flat on his face. I kicked Carter in the crotch and he bent over in a fit of agony, then they swarmed over me. I hit a man in the face and sent him spinning, his nose spurting blood, but after that I went down under sheer weight of numbers.

They yanked me off the floor, one man holding my right arm, another my left. I butted one of them in the face with my head. I kicked out with both feet at the cowboy in front of me, and then the men holding me forced me half down to the floor, jamming me there so I couldn't do anything effectively. Rome, running toward me from behind the counter, shouted, "Let me swing on him. He hit me this morning."

I wasn't more than half-conscious as a man slugged me in the face, but I held onto enough of my senses to hear Susan scream, "He knows where they went. Make him tell." And I glimpsed my father trying to get to me, calling, "Stop that, stop that," as if he were issuing an order to a band of recalcitrant school boys. Someone shoved him back against the wall. Then Rome was there, grinning like a small boy pulling wings off a captive fly. He hit me in the face, rocking it, and I spit at him.

Effie plowed through the crowd, shoving and pushing and cursing. She slapped one of the men holding me and kicked the other on the shin. "Let him go," she bellowed. "Let him go and he'll whip any three of you. What do you think you are, holding him while a pipsqueak like Rome hits him?"

They released me and scattered before her, some of them red in the face, Carter barely able to stand upright. He said, "You heard what he said, Effie. We don't have to listen to talk like that."

"It's true, ain't it?" Effie shot back. "Dick and Russ and everybody else who's got land on the creek had better listen. If a man gets hung for stealing, how about you, Jesse? Ain't rustling stealing? And you Bud. You can't go back to Wyoming. And you, O'Hara, keeping Billy Wrangel when you knew all the time what he was. I could go right on down the line, and half of you would get your necks stretched. I say let's wait till we get proof that Hardman and Logan done it." Out of the corner of her mouth, she said to me, "Drift."

But I wasn't ready yet. I wiped blood from my lips. The room was silent except for the sound of breathing and shuffling of feet. I said, "You go ahead and hang Hardman and Logan if you can catch them, but I'll tell you something. If you do, they'll sleep with you and eat with you and they'll ride in the saddle with you as long as you live."

I backed away into the street, hearing O'Hara shout, "We can't wait, Effie. We won't get our work done if we sit around here whistling for our money."

"They got mine, too, Mike," Effie said, "but I'd rather lose it than hang two men for something they didn't do."

I was out of the light then. I ran across the road to the hotel, calling, "Blow out the lamp, Judy." I didn't want her to see my face. When the room went dark, I stepped through the door and she was there, her arms around me.

"Are you all right, Bob? Are you all right?"

"Sure, sure. Now listen. Your dad's giving the orders like Effie said he would. They're dividing up and starting around the Hole, and they're going east from here. That means they'll stumble onto the cabin even if Mike doesn't think of it. You'll have to get Hardman and Logan out of there. I'll do more good if I go north. I'll be up on one of those ledges. If they're chasing you and it's close, I can slow them down."

She kissed me and tasted blood, and cried out, "Bob, you're hurt."

"I'm all right. Go on now."

I buckled my gun belt around me and picked up my rifle. We felt our way through the hotel to the back. I untied Judy's pony and helped her into the saddle, and waited until the sound of hoofs was lost to the east. I heard nothing from the store, so I swung into the saddle, satisfied that Judy was not being followed and turned toward the creek. I rode slowly, hoping they would not hear me, and followed the road toward Dick Smith's place.

By the time I reached the foot of the bandit trail, the sun was up. I had forgotten how it was here, with the sandstone cut back so that it resembled a giant staircase. Now I saw that Effie was right, that two men up there on a ledge could hold off an army. But it wasn't smart, either, for sooner or later whoever was forted up would have to come down. Still, it would buy time as Effie had said, and time might be the answer.

I ate the roast beef and the biscuits, and took a drink from my canteen. I left my buckskin behind a boulder at the foot of the trail, and with my Winchester in my hand, started to climb. I stopped when I reached a point where I had a good view of this end of the Hole and sat down, the sun even hotter that it had been the day before, or so it seemed.

Again I thought of my father, trying to help me as he shouted at them to stop. He wouldn't have done that last fall, but he wasn't the man he was then. Perhaps the shame he talked about had lifted him out of the world of books, had given him courage he had always lacked. But the real showdown was still ahead, and I wondered what he would do when it came.

27

AT MIDDAY the sun was an overheated furnace with nature's dampers wide open. No shade, no wind here on the ledge. Just stagnant heat, magnified by the sheer sandstone wall above and below me. I wasn't sweating. Not any more. I was sweated out, wrung dry.

I put my hand on my Winchester and jerked it away, my fingers and palm actually burned. I lay on the rifle to protect it from the sun, hoping it would cool enough so I could use it if I needed it when the time came, and looked south across the barren, boulder-strewn floor of the valley.

Two clouds of dust were visible. Three riders were kicking up the first dust, Hardman, Logan and Judy; the second cloud was larger. The riders made a dark mass, so far away I could not distinguish any of them, but I knew who they were too. Nineteen or twenty of them altogether, a small army with more than enough ropes to do the job. Not here, for none of the dwarf cedars at this end of the valley was big enough. No, they would go back to the settlement where the tall cottonwoods that lined the road had limbs as thick as a man's thighs.

I wiped my face with a hand that came away dry. I pulled my hat lower on my forehead. I felt the hot bulge of the rifle under me. Suddenly I could not stay on the ledge any longer. I had left my buckskin behind a tall boulder at the base of the cliff where he could not be seen by anyone riding from the south.

I picked up my rifle and walked down the twisting trail, which made two sharp switchbacks before it reached the base of the cliff. The Winchester was still hot but I could hold it without burning my hand. I leaned it against the boulder, thinking that when the time came, I would probably be using my hand gun instead of my rifle.

Then I heard them coming, the muffled thud of hoofs against the soft, dry earth, or the metallic crack of a shoe on stone. I stepped out of the boulder's shade into the harsh sunshine. They were close, strung out in Indian file: Hardman, then Logan, and Judy in the rear.

A minute later Eli Hardman reined up beside my horse and stepped down. He winked at me, picked up my canteen and took a drink, then wiped his mouth with his sleeve and put the canteen down. He knew what he was doing. He always did. He might have to sweat it out for hours with Logan up there above us somewhere on the side of the cliff where there wasn't a drop of water. He'd need every bit that was in his canteen.

"Them bastards are humping right along," he said. "Now that's what I call gratitude."

Sam Logan rode in a moment later. He dismounted and took a drink, waved my half-empty canteen back and forth as he listened to it slosh, then replaced it.

I admired Hardman, I thought, but I liked Logan. That was a big difference in the way I felt about them.

I said nothing until Judy reined up. I gave her a hand and she took it and stepped down. I put an arm around her and hugged her, and for just a moment I forgot the heat, and the danger that threatened Hardman and Logan, and the wild-eyed mob that wasn't far away. I forgot everything except that Judy was here and I loved her and she loved me.

"We ain't got a hell of a lot of time," Hardman said. "I figured we'd let our horses blow a minute, then start up the trail. Me and Sam won't have to go far. We'll knock a few of them out of their saddles before they know what hit 'em."

"After that the rest of 'em will lose their nerve," Logan added. "I'm aiming to get that damned Paul Rome with the first shot."

"No," I said. "That's not the way we're going to do it. You boys won't hang the way it stands now, but if you kill some of that bunch, you will. Besides, my father's with them. So's Judy's."

"Sounds like you're still figuring on taking us in."

147

"He won't take you in," Judy cried. "I promised you he wouldn't."

"This is my show and I aim to run it," I said. "Why do you think I came here—to cook in this damned heat?"

Hardman picked up my canteen and drank again. He said nothing.

"To keep that bunch of fools from hanging you," I said. "I owe you that much."

"And more," Judy said, tight-lipped.

"Another thing," I said. "I figured that if that bunch was right on your tail, I could slow them up with a little lead."

"They were closer for a while last night than they are now," Judy said. "We were slow getting out of the cabin."

I pointed to the ledge where I had spent most of the morning. "Get up there," I said. "The ledge widens out around that shoulder. There's plenty of room for your horses. Stay out of sight while I talk."

Hardman brushed one side of his mustache with his right hand, then the other side. He said, "Bob, you and Judy had best come with us. I know how crowds like that perform. They'll cut you down."

"Go on, go on," I urged. "You go with them, Judy."

"I'm staying here," she said. When she got a certain expression in her eyes and that hard set at the corners of her mouth, I knew there was no use arguing.

They swung up, Hardman saying, "Your funeral, son. They'll hang you high and the buzzards'll be pecking your eyes out in an hour. You'll see."

They started up the trail, neither looking back. I watched them for a moment, then turned to Judy, hearing the sound of oncoming horses. I took her hands and squeezed them, looking down at her.

I said, "I don't expect much help from Dad."

I wanted to say it would be her father who would set it off, and I'd kill him if I had to. That overpowering fear had been in me for hours. How could I marry Judy if I shot and killed her father?

"I think I can handle Mike," she said.

I thought she could too.

As I stood awaiting the mob in the pitiless sunshine, the

thought occurred to me that this was the final scene of a winter-long drama, this was the reaping of the crop that had grown through the winter.

I could not blame it all on Susan and Paul Rome, or upon the greed of Jesse Carter, or upon the willingness of these people to harbor outlaws and then turn against them when they needed a scapegoat. It was the result of all these things, including my own treachery; it was the sum total of man's sins and virtues, concentrated here in Dirken's Hole.

I stared at the mass of riders, my attention fixed on Mike O'Hara, but I could see Rome, his face red with fresh sunburn, trying to stetch his legs in the stirrups so he could rest a moment. I glimpsed my father in the rear of the party. He must, I thought, be far wearier than Rome.

Now, for some reason that puzzled me, he turned his horse and rode to one side, not stopping until he was thirty feet from the others. Susan, too, appeared puzzled by this maneuver. She was not the attractive woman she had been the night before. She sat slumped wearily over the horn with no trace of the proud posture characteristic of her.

Carter, fat toad that he was, sat his saddle like a sack of wool, content to permit O'Hara to keep the leadership he had assumed the night before.

They were close now. They stopped on the other side of the boulder, and I heard O'Hara call out, "We've got 'em boxed. They came down that trail last fall, but they ain't going back up. All we've got to do is to go after 'em and root 'em out."

Paul Rome said, "They've got the money on them. They must have."

I stepped into view, my gun lined on O'Hara. "You're staying here," I said.

My sudden appearance shocked them into immobility. They may have thought I was up there on the trail with Hardman and Logan. Or maybe their attention had been so closely fixed on the men they were after that they hadn't given me a thought. In any case, they didn't expect me to show up with a gun in my hand. They simply sat their heaving, sweat-gummed horses and stared at me.

The farmers, either by accident or design, had drawn off to the right and made a solid block. In all this group of about

149

twenty riders, only Effie was an ally. She was watching Susan. I don't know what she expected, but she was tense, as if she were ready to make a flying leap out of her saddle and drag Susan to the ground.

All of this I saw, or maybe sensed, for I had to watch O'Hara. Mike O'Hara was so choked up with anger he couldn't talk. I wanted to look at my father far in the rear, but I didn't dare take my eyes off O'Hara. He had been and still was the driving force, not Rome. I had been sure the day before that, if given enough time, both whiskey and desire would be worked out of most of them. Actually only four or five had anything tangible at stake. If I could somehow overpower O'Hara, I was reasonably sure the others would turn around and ride off.

I let the tension build until I thought it had reached its peak. Then I said, "I tried to tell you last night and all I got was a beating, but now I'll tell you again. You will not hang the two men you're after. You're not the law. You've purposely kept the law out of Dirken's Hole. Now turn around and start riding."

But O'Hara could not stand it any longer. He shouted, "You may be a big man outside the Hole, but you ain't here. We're going up that trail until we find our men. I'm gonna count three and that's it."

This was what I had been afraid of. O'Hara had a stubborn courage and pride, and I actually think he would have let me kill him rather than back down at this point. But I was counting on Judy and she didn't let me down. She called from the top of the boulder, "Don't do it, Mike. I'll shoot Rome and Bob will shoot you. Is it worth it?"

Their heads tipped back to see her. I don't think any of them knew she was with me. Certainly O'Hara, judging from the paralysis that seized him, didn't know. His face went from red to purple, turning so dark I thought he would have a stroke. All he could say was, "You, too?"

"Me too," Judy said. "The man you want has been riding with you. Why don't you take him?"

"That's right." It was my father's voice.

He sat his saddle, thin and tall and straight-backed. His face was very pale, whether from utter weariness or fear I could not tell. At this moment he was a stranger to me, ca-

150

pable of doing things I would have said were impossible a few months ago. They looked at him, Susan open-mouthed, Rome so nervous he was trembling, the rest simply astonished.

"I would have told you sooner," my father went on, "but you weren't ready for it. I wasn't either. No man likes to talk about his own personal disgrace."

"Shut up, Tom," Susan cried.

"The money is in a drawer in a bureau in my house," my father said. "Hardman and Logan didn't take it."

So this was the way he expected to stop Susan and Rome. He had waited almost too long. He should have talked up last night, but maybe fear had held him, or maybe he hoped that some miracle would keep his shame from being exposed. Or possibly he thought they would not listen to him. Even now they weren't sure.

Finally O'Hara asked, "Are you asking us to believe you stole it?"

"No," my father said. "It was stolen by——"

A gun shot stopped him. With stupifying horror I saw my father crumple and fall out of his saddle as his frightened horse reared and spun away. Everyone seemed to be held by the same horror that shocked me. I was the first to recover, I saw the smoking gun in Rome's hand, and I shot him twice. Both bullets caught him in the chest. He must have been dead before he fell to the ground.

Chaos then, with men yelling and horses whirling, and Susan putting hers into a run trying to get away, but Effie was faster. She overtook Susan and grabbing her by an arm, tumbled her out of the saddle. Effie fell on top of her, hitting her on one side of the face and then the other. Susan lay on her back, her skirt flying as she cursed and kicked and tried to scratch Effie's face, but Effie was merciless. She beat Susan into submission, hitting her until an eye was closed and blood ran down into her mouth from her nose.

I rammed through the crowd of men and horses to my father who lay on his back, a hand pressed against his chest, O'Hara bent over him, shouting, "Did you tell the truth, Tom?"

Dick Smith pulled O'Hara back, saying, "A dying man don't lie, Mike. You know that."

I knelt by my father's side as I heard Effie say to Susan,

"Tell 'em, you bitch, or I'll whop you silly. Is the money where he said it was?"

"It's there," Susan said in a muffled voice. Her lips were too bruised for her to talk clearly. "Paul took it from the safe and I hid it. I didn't think Tom knew."

Judy was there, then, kneeling on the other side of my father. "It's all right, Mr. Buel. We'll get you to the hotel. Effie's a good doctor."

A smile was on my father's pale lips. "It's no good, Judy. I told Robert the other night. I've heard men who fought in the Civil War tell about their friends having premonitions before they went into battle. I guess that was what I had. I'm not afraid. It's time for me."

Tears ran down my face. I could not talk. My father raised a hand searching for mine and I took it. He said, "Robert, Robert, it's all right. I'm proud of myself at last. I did one good thing in all these years when I should have done so many."

"You have a right to be proud," Judy said softly.

And I found my voice enough to say, "You're a brave man."

"That's a compliment, coming from you, Robert," he said. "I used to tremble at some of the things you did. I wish . . . I wish we could have been a little closer." He squeezed my hand, and then he said, "Robert, I'd like to be buried beside your mother."

A moment later he was gone, his hand suddenly slack in mine, and I rose and turned away, unable to escape the feeling that it was my fault this had happened. I should have been watching Rome. But I hadn't expected it from him. I hadn't even expected my father to say what he had. Still, I should have been watching, for I knew that no man, least of all Paul Rome, was entirely predictable.

Judy touched my arm. When I looked back, I saw that Effie had brought a saddle blanket and covered my father's body. Carter and his crew had ridden away. The farmers stood in a group looking at me. O'Hara was twenty feet from them, staring at the ground. Effie went back to stand over Susan, who sat with her bruised face in her hands, whimpering like a child.

"Bob," Judy said, "I'm to blame. I was watching Rome. I

should have shot him before he got his gun out, but after your father started talking, I just couldn't seem to move."

I put an arm around her, knowing that neither of us should blame ourselves. I said, "He wanted to die. It was the only way he could find peace. I don't think he knew any peace from the moment my mother died."

The farmers came to us, Dick Smith in the lead. He held out his hand to me. "We've been talking," he said. "We want to shake hands with you. We should of known about Carter and Rome. It's plain enough now, but I reckon a man just kind o' gets into a way of thinking and acting."

So I shook hands with them, Smith and Musil and Dale Oren's oldest boy and the rest, and all the time, I was wondering if the system of peonage that existed between them and Jesse Carter would ever change. When we finished, Smith said, "We'll take the body in and we'll build a coffin. We'll dig the grave if you'll tell us where he wanted to be buried."

"I'll show you in the morning," I said. "It's in the other end of the Hole. Beside my mother."

"I know the place," Musil said. "We'll take care of it this afternoon. We'd better have the funeral tomorrow. This heat, you know."

I nodded and walked away, to the other side of the boulder where I had left my horse and my Winchester. I still had a job to do and I wasn't looking forward to it with any pleasure. Hardman and Logan were up there on that ledge above me, and they knew I'd be coming after them.

But O'Hara followed me. He said, "Buel," in a commanding tone. I turned, one hand on the barrel of my Winchester. He stood there, his stubby legs spread, his mottled face still more purple than red. He looked as much like a cutlass-swinging pirate as ever. He said, "I never forgive a man. I ain't starting today. You've done me more hurt than any man living and now you're taking Judy away from me."

"That's right." Funny, I thought. I couldn't hate him. In a way I admired him. At least I did not feel toward him as I did Jesse Carter. I added, "You've still got your sheep."

He clenched his fists, and a little breath of wind tugged at his beard. He said, "By God, you'd better take care of my girl. That's all I've got to say."

153

"You worry about your sheep, O'Hara," I said. "I'll take care of my wife."

He wheeled and stomped away. As I picked up my rifle, Judy said, "No, Bob." She pointed toward the crest of the north rim far above the ledge where I expected to find Hardman and Logan. For a moment they were sillhouetted against the hot, blue sky. They waved their hats in what would be, for Hardman at least, a derisive gesture.

I was too shocked to say anything except, "Everybody told me this was a one-way trail."

"We all thought it was," Judy said. "Even Dad. Billy Wrangel never told him any different if he knew. Maybe he didn't. You know how it is with men like Hardman and Logan. They don't tell their secrets, but coming here this morning, I overheard enough to know what they were going to do."

"But how did they get up there?" I asked. "That ledge I was on had a dead end."

"I suppose they didn't follow that ledge," she said. "It's like a puzzle. You've got to take the right turn every time. There's some dangerous jumps to make, and you know how they train their horses. They didn't want to go this way. They intended to go over the pass. That's why they went to the rock cabin first."

I stood there, staring at the sky, my hand still clutching my rifle barrel. So I could not keep my bargain, for it would be useless to try to follow the trail they had taken. In a way I was glad it had gone this way. I had no desire to shoot it out with them until I was dead, or they were dead, and that's the way it would have been. There could have been no compromise for either of us.

"Forgive me," Judy said nervously. "I couldn't tell you what they intended to do or you wouldn't have let them. This way the lawmen will get them. That's the reason they wanted to go over the pass. They've seen the Rock Springs sheriff and some deputies on the rim a couple of times and they were afraid they'd run into them."

"If they don't," I said, "the railroad will lose fifty thousand dollars."

"No it won't," Effie called. "They never took a look at their saddle bags. I filled 'em with newspapers yesterday morning

154

when I came back from the store. Them greenbacks are under the mattress in their room."

I shook my head at Effie, completely puzzled. "Isn't it a little late for you to be getting religion?"

"Something's got to be done to keep them boogers out of here," she said. "Hardman and Logan ain't gonna ride back into the Hole after this ruckus, and word's gonna get around about what happened to that dinero." She stuck out her lower lip at me. "I can read the writing on the wall. Either we clean up our own mess or some bastard like Harwig will do it for us."

She whirled and walked off to stare down at Susan who was still on the ground. She said, "Get up, you bitch. We're riding. As soon as the pass is open, we're riding again. Right to the nearest jail."

"She'll do it, too," Judy said to me. "She'd rather go to the law than have the law come here."

"Dirken's Hole will never be the same after today," I said.

"You did it." She put her hands on my shoulders, looking up at me. "And you're going to do something else. You're going to show me the White River country."

"A pleasure," I said.

Ride into the WILD WILD west with Ballantine Westerns and...

LEE LEIGHTON